Other Calista Jacobs mysteries
by Kathryn Lasky Knight

*Mumbo Jumbo*
*Mortal Words*
*Trace Elements*

As Kathryn Lasky, the author has written numerous
children's books.

# Dark Swan

Kathryn Lasky Knight

St. Martin's Press
New York

*Design by Junie Lee*

Knight, Kathryn Lasky.
    Dark swan / Kathryn Lasky Knight.
      p.  cm.
    "A Thomas Dunne book."
    ISBN 0-312-10961-X
    1. Jacobs, Calista (Fictitious character)—Fiction.  2. Jacobs, Charley
(Fictitious character)—Fiction.  3. Mothers and sons—Massachusetts—
Boston—Fiction.  4. Women  artists—Massachusetts—Boston—Fic-
tion.  5. Teenage boys—Massachusetts—Boston—Fiction.  6. Boston
(Mass.)—Fiction.  I. Title.
PS3561.N485D37   1994
813'.54—dc20                                      94-601
                                                                   CIP

First edition: July 1994

10 9 8 7 6 5 4 3 2 1

The violence of the gesture seemed entirely out of scale with the tools or the object. But Mrs. Elliot Kingsley obviously knew what she was doing as she stabbed the chopsticks into the tiny, tenacious roots. For this needle juniper, barely two feet high, was eighty years old.

"Mrs. Kingsley Senior gave it to me when I became engaged to Kingie. That was almost sixty years ago. The juniper and I are the same age." This Mrs. Kingsley, Quintana, looked up and smiled at Calista Jacobs, who was perched on a stool in the greenhouse and sketching madly, quick little smudgy drawings with graphite pencils or in some cases, when she wanted something more precise yet loose, she'd pull out her Rapidograph pen. She smiled quietly to herself. What was it about these old Brahmins that compelled them to call their own mothers-in-law Mrs.? Thank God that Archie's parents weren't that way. She couldn't imagine calling Nan and Will Mr. and Mrs. Baldwin. Of course, they were not her in-laws. In fact, they cheerfully referred to themselves as Calista's outlaws. Still, despite the Baldwins' impeccable pedigree, they had none of the oppressive formality that one could encounter on the North Shore, Dedham, or up here on Beacon Hill—where only a few of the truly old guard remained.

"Now I take my little scissors here. They tell me these are very similar to what cardiovascular surgeons use in open-heart surgery. . . ." Quintana was bending over the plant with her reading glasses sliding down her nose and making expert little cuts. Calista could hear the sound of the needles being snipped. "Oh! Got to nip that bud. Hand me those shears over there, dear." She pointed to scaled-down needlenose shears with gleaming edges. Calista handed them over. "I call these 'Old Reliable.' You get a nice clean angled cut with them, and these buds tend to be quite fibrous. This old dear would just shoot completely out of bounds if that was allowed." There was a small crunching sound. Calista winced. This was an art form definitely not to her inclination.

"You will note, Calista, that the emphasis in the word *bonsai* is on the second syllable, *sai*. It is the verb meaning 'to grow.' " Calista blinked, the blink of irony mingled with disbelief, as she looked at the scores of dwarfed plants surrounding her in the greenhouse. "The *bon*," Quintana Kingsley continued, "refers to the salver or tray in which they are grown. And now for the mighty little shears!"

The old woman picked up a set of shears that came as close to looking like a piranha's jaws as anything else and began paring away at some of the exposed roots near the trunk of the juniper. Calista bit her lip and turned to observe another tree, a Japanese zelkova with faint pink leaves the size of babies' fingernails. It was the tree, after all, in which the emperor's nightingale first sings.

Calista, a distinguished children's book illustrator, had been working for months now on the illustrations for her next book—a retelling of the classic fairy tale *The Emperor and the Nightingale*. She had pored over books of Oriental landscape design at Boston's Horticultural Hall and spent hours at Harvard's Fogg Museum studying the exquisite seventeenth-century painted scrolls, but what had helped her the most was purely serendipitous. She had had to move temporarily into Nan and Will Baldwin's Louisburg Square house while her own was undergoing extensive work. It was impossible to concentrate with the pounding of five guys crawling on her roof to reshingle, not to mention the addition of a sunroom, which in her more high-blown moments she thought of as a conservatory. But Calista was neither a musician nor a particularly good indoor gardener. The whole notion of the sunroom had started when her mother had given her a camellia. It had survived admirably until the very day they began work on the new room. Was it the plaster dust, the trauma of the sledgehammers knocking out a wall where the new room would be added? Or had she mortally offended the plant's soul in some way? Was that plant saying to her, I'm a good old Yankee camellia. I don't need special treatment, a room of my own—what an extravagance!

Calista spent money—freely, if one didn't count the price of the guilt. She had most likely transferred some of that guilt to the plant, so that it began to shrivel on the day the workmen came and five days later was dead.

Calista and her son, Charley, soon had had it with the chaos of construction and sought refuge at the Baldwins' on Louisburg Square. Nan and Will were the parents of Calista's lover, Archie. Archie, an archaeologist who held a joint appointment at Harvard and the Smithsonian, was away on a dig. Calista would have liked to have been with him, but she was late on this book, which in turn was making her late on the next. So this was her summer to get things done. It had worked out quite well actually, as the Baldwins were at their summer place on Mount Desert Island in Maine, and Heckie, their faithful manservant, who usually took care of things in Boston, had suffered a stroke.

Therefore, when Calista asked whether she might retreat to 16 Louisburg Square, Nan and Will were only too happy to have her there watering plants, taking care of the cats, and generally looking out for things. Charley, Calista's son, had a summer job working on the swan boats in the Public Garden, a mere seven-minute walk from the front door of number 16. And then when Calista discovered that her next-door neighbor Quintana Kingsley had a black belt in bonsai and she saw the extraordinary collection of plants—said to be worth hundreds of thousands of dollars—she realized the landscape for *The Emperor and the Nightingale* was all right there, next door at number 18! She would never have to go to the libraries again for research on this book.

Mrs. Kingsley, or Queenie, as she was called, although the other part of her matched name set, her husband, Kingie, had died some years before, was thrilled that her dear little trees were being immortalized in a fairy tale by the famous illustrator. "A consummation, indeed, devoutly to be wished," she had exclaimed.

Consummation all around, Calista thought, if one did not include the absence of sex, what with Archie being so far afield. But it was all so convenient—the proximity of Charley's job, the ready-made Oriental landscape, the escape from the noise and dust of construction. Calista did hope to get up to her vacation home in Vermont. So far, however, she had been working too hard. On occasion, she did miss Cambridge—but it was just across the river and she and Charley were always popping over for dinner and books. She was used to the Cambridge bookshops. In certain areas, Calista did not tolerate change well.

She now began to pack up her drawing equipment. "I better be going, Quintana." She could not bring herself to call her Queenie. At first, she had called her Mrs. Kingsley, but this apparently was not necessary unless one was a daughter-in-law or a servant.

"Oh, my dear, I enjoy our visits so much." Quintana straightened up now, with another, even smaller pair of shears in hand, and took off her glasses. Amazing what glasses could do for a certain kind of face. Without them, Quintana Kingsley looked remarkably bland and . . . well, yes, no mental giant. But that was not it, really. Without her glasses, she looked like a very old baby. There was a kind of innocence in her eyes that did not match the stringy neck and the mouth pleated with little vertical lines that made it seem as if her lips were on drawstrings.

"Well, Charley will be home soon from the swan boats."

"Oh!" The older woman touched her thin gray hair as if to jump-start a few neurons under the skull. "That reminds me! I think this job of his sounds marvelous—the swan boats. How lovely. You know my grandson, Jamie, he needs something like that. He's been down in the dumps for weeks now—refuses to go out to the country club for tennis. Refused to go to summer school to make up a poor grade in math. . . . So I don't know what'll happen there . . . I mean, I suppose Harvard will take him. . . . They always have. . . ." She looked vaguely over at a small pine bent nearly double in a strangely arthritic posture.

It took Calista a minute to fathom what Quintana had meant when she'd said "They always have." But, of course, this was the way it was with so many of these old families—a steady stream of males, and now females, passing through Harvard, generation after generation. Their children could have abysmal SAT scores and lousy grades, but they would still get in. With an intensive-care unit of round-the-clock tutors and sympathetic housemasters, they limped through. Getting in was the hard part, anyhow, at Harvard. Staying in was no great trick. And Harvard needed these families' money. The blood often thinned before the money. The brain tissue might be a bit frayed around the edges, but they were still good for a few more generations of giving. Calista was sure that many Kingsleys over the years with less than shimmering intellects had passed through with the requisite gentlemen C's. The idea was to pick and choose carefully in terms of curriculum and to avoid at all costs particle-physics courses like the ones that Calista's late husband had taught.

"Well, how old is Jamie?"

"Oh, he'll just be a junior in high school. But I think he needs to do something—you know it will look poorly on his application if he has no extracurricular or summer activities to list. So I was wondering whether perhaps your son, Charley, might take him round, show him the swan boats. Perhaps there's an opening."

"Well, I doubt it. Those jobs are very coveted. Charley, I

think, went in last November. But you never know. I'll ask him about it."

"Oh thank you, dear. That's so sweet of you. Now can you find your way out?"

"Of course."

Calista walked out of the greenhouse, through a potting-shed area, and then into a back-hall region that was a nineteenth-century maze of old storage rooms—sculleries, butler's pantries, immense china closets, and silver vaults. She made her way down a putty-colored hallway that led directly into the kitchen. Funny, she had not really noticed the framed pictures on the wall before. They were children's drawings. She stopped now to look. They were nice. She could tell by the paper that they had been done many years ago by some Kingsley child—now grown up, most likely. There were the familiar stick figures standing in front of tall peaked-roof houses and often stiff little rows of flowers perched atop a line to represent earth. They were very typical of a child's early drawings—similar certainly to the ones Charley had done around the age of four or five. After he got the basic family figures down pat, he had moved on to dinosaurs and fast cars in his artwork. But there was something odd here. Did this child— or children, for there seemed to be more than one artist—have the family members down pat? What was strange? Calista stepped closer. None of them had hands! That was it. How very curious. Just then she heard a "Yoo-hoo" coming from the kitchen. A tall figure of a woman suddenly lunged through the pantry and into the hall.

"Oh!" She looked slightly appalled and covered her mouth as she saw Calista standing in front of the drawings.

"Oh, I'm sorry. I didn't mean to startle you. I'm Calista Jacobs and I was just over here . . ."

"Oh, I know. Yes, Mother told me all about you. You're Archie Baldwin's friend. I'm Bootsie McPhee." She had wonderful celadon green eyes. They were slightly elongated and tipped down a bit at the far corners, which gave them a natural gravity that was distancing but not forbidding. These were the eyes of a very private person, Calista thought.

"How nice to meet you," Calista said. And both women shot out their hands, which collided awkwardly in a kind of glancing blow rather than a handshake. They laughed and tried again. "This is your artwork here?"

"Yes, and my sister's, as well. At one time, I actually had aspirations of being an artist, but it kind of petered out, I guess."

Petered out along with the hands, Calista thought. The more she looked at these drawings, the more interesting they became. They blended a kind of stasis and movement that was very puzzling. "I think they're rather good," Calista said suddenly. "I think maybe you should have stuck with it."

"Well, I take that as a compliment. I am familiar with your books. I read many of them to my son, Jamie."

"But didn't your mother tell me that you do something with art? Isn't that right? Art history?"

"Oh, not very seriously—museum stuff within the area of Japanese art and the China Trade." She paused and inhaled sharply. "I love your name—Calista, lovely name." This was a non sequitur that Calista couldn't quite follow. "What does it mean? Is it Italian?"

"No, Greek, actually. It means happiness."

"Are you part Greek?"

"Oh no. My mother just liked the name."

"Just liked the name," Bootsie said musingly. "How nice. Bootsie's such a silly name, isn't it?"

"Oh . . ." Calista was at a loss for words. Was it a silly name? She guessed maybe so, and then Bootsie articulated the very thought lurking around her brain. "It's just not really a name, is it? I mean, for a human. You have a real name." Bootsie paused, then continued in a more reflective voice. "It's a bad habit, isn't it, in families like ours?"

"You mean the name?"

"Names," Bootsie replied with a sardonic grin. "My sister,

Muffy, was really Margaret. Mine is Barbara. I have a cousin Elizabeth, who's called Bambi, and then there's her sister Frances, or Fluff."

"Is it something they do only to girls?" Calista asked.

"Yes, boys manage to stay intact for the most part. Their names, that is." She smiled briefly, running her fingers through her hair. "Well, I'd better get out to Mummy." She continued down the hall.

Mummy, thought Calista. That was the other peculiarity of impeccably pedigreed upper-crust girls and women. Now why in heaven's name would a handsome woman like Bootsie with all that commanding bone structure and honey-colored hair—good grief, she looked an awful lot like Lauren Bacall—why would she call her mother Mummy? Whom was she trying to convince of her affection? In Calista's mind, it was an affectation of affection, a confection, if you will, of affection. She tried to imagine Charley calling her Mummy. It was ridiculous. He usually called her Mom. Sometimes he called her "Peahead" when she had her hair pulled back tightly, which wasn't often. And in damp weather, when her masses of silvery chestnut hair frizzed up, he called her "Tiggy," short for Mrs. Tiggy-Winkle, the hedgehog immortalized by Beatrix Potter.

Calista paused for another half minute in front of the drawings. It wasn't just that the hands were unfinished, nor did the arms simply dissolve into nothingness. No. There were straight lines across the wrists. There was no doubt about it: These hands had been chopped off intentionally.

# 2

The corn bread was warm and the beer came in long-necked bottles just the way Calista liked it, but a sudden and decided crinkling of the brow on his mother's face indicated to Charley something less than savory as she sat across from him. They were in their favorite barbecue joint, Red Bones in Davis Square in Somerville. Although it was next door to Cambridge, Somerville was definitely more town than gown. The noise and heat of the restaurant swirled around them as Calista read Charley's better-late-than-never term paper that would solve his "incomplete" situation in English.

"You don't like it?" Charley asked.

"Is this one of these male-bonding things? You know what I think of Robert Bly and all that beating your primal tom-tom crap."

"No, Mom. I got the idea from Archie. It's just what the title says, 'Dawn's Early Eats: An Analysis of the Upper Paleolithic Palate.' "

"Sounds like guys in groups eating red meat to me." Just then the waitress arrived and slid a plate of pulled pork topped with coleslaw, onions, and pickles in front of Calista.

"Irony!" Charley said slyly.

"What . . . huh?" Calista looked up from the term paper over the top of her reading glasses.

"I said that's irony." Charley nodded toward the meat in front of Calista. The waitress then put down an immense platter of Arkansas ribs in front of Charley. "Double irony," he said, smiling like the cat who had just eaten the canary rather than the adolescent about to tuck into a mound of pig ribs.

"Oh, the meat!" Calista said, finally getting it.

"See, you think I'm just a tech weenie and don't know about these arcane things like figures of speech and devices of literary style. I know what they are and I can use them in context. You say guys eating red meat and I say—"

"Okay, okay." Calista cut him off. "I get it—very clever, very appropriate. And it's not that I think you're a tech weenie. It was just that when that cousin of Archie's who teaches Shakespeare came over and you said, 'A whole semester for Shakespeare!' as if you thought it could be done in a weekend workshop or something. Well, it was kind of embarrassing, and then when I found out about this incomplete, I really did begin to worry about the humanities side of your education."

"I didn't take one computer course the entire year, Mom."

"There's none left for you to take at the high school, or math courses, either, for that matter."

Charley Jacobs took after his late father, Tom Jacobs, who had been a preeminent theoretical physicist at Harvard. Gifted in mathematics, a computer whiz by the end of his freshman year, Charley had exhausted what the public high school had to offer in terms of math and computers. Now just finishing tenth grade, he had taken a fractals and chaos theory course at MIT, but at his mother's request, he had also signed up for extra art courses at the high school—and had enjoyed them immensely, especially printmaking. Some way or other, however, Charley had neglected to hand in a final term paper for his English composition course.

He claimed it was an oversight. Calista was not sure how a term paper that counted a quarter of the grade became an oversight, but she had been ticked. Now she had to admit that despite the facetious tone of this paper—"In days of yore, when cholesterol was not a dirty word and jogging was for real"—Charley's effort was substantial and the paper was coherent—so far, no run-on sentences or comma splices. There was an automatic ten points off for that.

"This isn't bad . . . not bad, Charley." Calista put the paper into her bag so as not to stain it with the barbecue.

Charley was gnawing on a bone. On his upper lip, there was barbecue sauce that was the same color as his hair—red—and in the same place where his mustache had begun to show a shadow. She wasn't ready for this. A son who could shave. No more chortly baby face, triple chins, and all that. No more scrappy little boy. There was this rather lanky young man across the table from her with interesting angles in his face and a smart but hardly wise look in his eye. Babies' eyes were full of innocence, flecked sometimes with wisdom; yes, babies could on occasion look almost like sages. Adolescent eyes seemed masked by comparison. They were not innocent; yet they were far from knowing. Calista had looked hard into the eyes of Charley and those of his friends. When the masks lifted, there was an unsettling mixture of distrust and hope. It was of paramount importance for kids of this age never to let the hope show through, not even a glimmer. It was bad form to be caught out with hope in your eyes. It was really a balancing act. Of course, that was what all of adolescence added up to—an incredible, nerve-racking balancing act. Thank heavens Charley had a sense of humor. For both parent and child, negotiating the shoals and drafts of adolescence without humor would be the absolute pits.

They finished dinner and headed back to Boston and Beacon Hill. As she let herself and Charley into the quiet darkness of the Baldwins' home and stepped into the front room, as they called it, Calista always thought of a description she had read in *George*

*Santayana's America* of a Beacon Hill home, in which he described so eloquently the "solemnity and hush," a world of thick carpets and monumental furniture "heavy and fixed like sepulchers," and armchairs that "grew in their places like separate oaks."

And, of course, recumbent in that armchair was not Will Baldwin but Nestor, the goddamn cat. And on a Duncan Phyfe couch in a pose worthy of Madame Récamier herself was Ophelia, the other cat. Together, they constituted the only fly in the ointment of 16 Louisburg Square. Now, it was not that Calista had anything against cats. She didn't. Calista was simply not a cat person. She knew that the world was divided into those who were and those who were not. And she understood intimately the world of the cat person, because it just so happened that a lot of people in children's book publishing were cat people. Her editor, Janet Weiss, for one and her art director. But even Nestor and Ophelia might try the patience of Janet and Michael.

"Did you give them their sherry yet, Mom?"

"Yes, and Ophelia left a lot of hers, I see. She must be onto the fact that I'm watering it down." Ophelia slowly turned her head. Her luminous jade eyes bore into Calista: *Fool who would water down Hawker's amontillado?* It was all there in her eyes. No doubt about it.

Nan and Will had left a full page of notes concerning the cats. Sherry was one of their requisite snacks—although the vet had suggested watering down Ophelia's because of a chronic bladder problem. And Ophelia, in all her feline arrogance, seemed to be letting Calista know what she thought of this.

Nestor, not so arrogant, was just plain old mean and arthritic. So if she could get him fairly tight each night, he did seem a tad more pleasant in the morning. Nestor now rose from the mighty chair that grew like an oak, smirked at Calista, then languidly made his way toward the hearth, where he had the audacity to sniff at the chipped Royal Dalton saucer of adulterated sherry and walk away. This would all be quite touching if Nestor wasn't

such a wanton son of a bitch in his behavior toward Ophelia—despite the fact that Nan and Will were convinced that the cats never really fought and indeed loved each other dearly, devotedly. Hah! Calista had seen old Nestor tomcatting around in the connected gardens, trying out upper-crust pussy, as it were. And once when Ophelia had a nice fish head that she had gotten from the alley out back, Nestor, the lout, pounced right on her. Some love match!

Nan and Will had a blind spot with cats. They also, to Calista's mind, tended to overname them. The predecessors to this couple had been Eleanor and Franklin. But Calista just called these two Piss and Moan, because that was basically what they did all day long.

"You shouldn't have said that thing about the sherry out loud, Mom," Charley said, studying Nestor. "They both understood, and look at poor Piss limping over there to console her."

"So you think they're in love, too?"

"Piss and Moan?"

"Yeah."

"I don't know."

"Well, let's go to bed. You have an early date with the swans and I might have a nightcap on the back balcony while contemplating the mysteries of feline love."

# 3

Another perk of the house was the little balcony off Nan and Will's dressing room. It reminded Calista of a small afterdeck on a ship with a wrought-iron taffrail. There was a fairly decrepit but comfortable lounge chair and from this vantage a view of the Charles was afforded, if one was to look straight out; and if straight down, the Connecting Gardens were visible. These six contiguous gardens behind Louisburg Square had been formed in 1929, when the owners of the homes on the square and the two side streets decided to tear down the walls separating their small yards in order to create a larger space. The various gardens still emerged as separate entities through the construction of low walls and hedges. But the overall effect was one of unity and harmony.

The moon was full tonight and the plots thick with shade plantings. Ivy, hosta, and varieties of mosses were punctuated in the moonlight by occasional splashes of woodland flowers. There was a luxury of growth balanced with simplicity and perfect scale. Calista loved her perch above it all. She had poured herself a tumbler of seltzer and put in a splash of Grand Marnier. The moon was so bright, she barely needed her reading light. She was rereading *Barchester Towers*. She settled back and extended her legs delicately in a pose perhaps reminiscent of Signora Neroni, a character in the Trollope novel. La Signora Madeline Vesey Neroni was one of Calista's all-time literary favorites. With her mutilated legs that required her to be carried everywhere and then deposited on various chaises, the beautiful but crippled Madeline in her Grecian head bandeau and Empire gowns was a source of endless charm. So Calista skipped back a few pages to her favorite part—La Signora's entrance to a reception at the bishop's house. The fair lady was carried in from her carriage by shoals of attendants—an Italian manservant, a lady's maid, a page. It was a "perfect commotion" and "in this way they climbed easily into the drawing room. . . . the signora rested safely on her couch."

Calista delighted in this prose. Trollope was to writing what Randolph Caldecott was to drawing. Her favorite line perhaps in the whole book was when La Signora referred to her small daughter as having the blood of Tiberius flowing in her veins. "She is the last of the Neros." And then Trollope's wonderful disquisition on the peculiar phrase through the eyes of the bishop, who thinks that indeed he had heard "of the last of the Visigoths and the last of the Mohicans, but to have the last of the Neros thus brought before him for a blessing was very staggering." This was a shining moment in nineteenth-century wit and irony. Now this truly was irony, Calista thought, recalling Charley's reference to the pulled pork and Arkansas ribs. She wondered whether Charley was ready for Trollope. Fat chance!

She read for half an hour, enjoying every moment as the porcelain wit and charm of Trollope's words washed over her. She should really get to bed. She wanted to make one last drawing at Quintana's and had promised to be there as soon as she got Charley off to the swan boats. There was still a light on in the Kingsleys' greenhouse. She had hoped Archie would call tonight. But it was very hard for him to get to a phone down there in

Guatamala. He had written her one fabulously sexy letter in which he had told a story about a strangely beautiful flower that grew in the rain forest where he was working. He described the anatomical charms it possessed to lure a particular hummingbird to its nectar, its nectar being particularly sweet and held in a cup within a cluster. Oh Lord, it made her horny just to think about it. Well, he'd be back in a few more weeks.

Calista went to bed. She thought about her conservatory. She would try some more camellias, and maybe some strange small orchids with parts like females. They were so exotic. A mini rain forest in the dead of winter in Cambridge was appealing. She tried to imagine bromeliads, pink and spiky, in the drab New England January. She had read about tank bromeliads in the rain forest that held gallons of water and became small aquatic worlds, containing a life of their own with frogs and salamanders. Worlds within worlds, rather like multiple-universe theories. That was what Tom had just started to toy with at the time of his death—black holes and multiple universes, and strings and wormholes as corridors to simultaneous universes. He and Hawking had just begun to correspond and then . . .

Calista fell asleep thinking about gravity and black holes, bromeliads and orchids—orchids with spilling cups of nectar.

It must have been around three in the morning. The screeching tore like claws on the silk of the night. Calista opened her eyes wide. A terrible screaming seared the air. "Fucking cats!" she muttered. She rolled over and tried to go back to sleep. They kept the screeching up. She got out of bed and walked through the dressing room and looked down on the Connecting Gardens. There they were, the two of them standing on a low stone wall, wailing to beat the band. This was more than just the sherry. Nestor was absolutely prancing around, looking quite unarthritic.

Calista went downstairs muttering. She poured two saucers of milk laced with sherry. She stepped out the back door. "Come on, kitty, kitty." The cats came running. This sudden obedience startled her. Neither cats, children, nor lovers had ever responded with so much alacrity. She went back upstairs, amazed to see them following her.

"Oh no, guys. You're not sleeping with me." She scooped them up and took them into the breakfast room, where their cat beds were, and deposited them. They looked up at her with an alarming mixture of contrition and respect.

Calista went back to bed and fell asleep with the disturbing thought that the cats might begin to like her, become attached in some way.

# 4

"Listen to this, Piss." Calista was in the breakfast room with her first cup of coffee.

"You talking to the cats, Tiggy?" Charley said as he came in, his hair still wet from the shower. Calista's had frizzed in the heavy humidity of the morning.

"Yeah, last night they had bad dreams or something and I had to get them in from the gardens. They were actually very nice to me. But this morning, Piss is as ornery as ever. I'm just reading this rather interesting little piece buried on page seven of the *Globe*."

"Which is?" Charley popped a bagel in the toaster.

"Okay, listen up, Piss. Dateline Edwards, Tennessee. 'A devoted couple who died within seconds of each other in a nursing home were buried on the day that would have been their seventy-fifth wedding anniversary. Luke and Dot Peters died while side by side in single beds in the Pleasant Meadow nursing home. Both were ninety-five years old. "It was almost simultaneous," said Dr. Louis Matchen. A nurse reported that Dot stopped breathing and then she heard Luke give a short gasp. Luke Peters had been comatose for a week and would not have known of his wife's death, but the couple had repeatedly said that they wanted to die together.' " Calista looked over the top of the newspaper at Piss, who was trying to stretch his creaking back. Moan was whimpering in her basket. "Isn't that sweet, Piss?" Calista asked. The cat didn't even look at her. "I'm worried about Moan. She really hasn't eaten anything for two days. The doctor said it wasn't really worth it to do that laser stuff with her bladder."

"So you think she might kick—buy the farm—and you're hoping that Piss will go with her?" Charley asked.

"Well, I just thought it was a touching story."

"Piss doesn't."

"Guess not." She watched him waddle off toward the cat-treat bag on a corner shelf, then look directly at Charley.

"Okay, okay, I'm a-coming." Charley got up and poured some into a bowl. "Ooh, I'm late. I got to be going."

"Well, take that bagel with you. You don't eat enough. I don't see how you pedal halfway round the pond on what you eat."

Calista cleared up the breakfast dishes and went upstairs to shower. There was no hope for her hair on a day like this. It was already kinking madly as she piled it wet on top of her head. She looked out the window. The skies looked just like gefilte fish— lumpy and gray. And there was a heavy low-tide smell in the air, the way Boston always smelled when the wind came in from the southeast on a warm summer day. She put on a pair of shorts, a T-shirt, flip-flops and grabbed her bag with her pencils, pens, and drawing pad. She went back downstairs and out the Baldwins' back door, for she knew Quintana would already be at work and not hear the front doorbell ring. She crossed their terrace, went down two steps into another garden, across it, then up into the Kingsleys'. There was a small stone squirrel perched under a seedling oak surrounded by carpets of ivy and edged with red-and-white trillium that backed up to the greenhouse. The door was on the other side. Calista walked around and went in.

"Quin . . ." The sound died on her lips. At first, she saw the juniper, its salver broken on the floor. But Quintana Kingsley could never have been mistaken for being asleep. Her head was cocked at an angle no living, breathing person could sustain. A thin thread of blood had dried in a jagged line from the corner of her mouth to her chin. Her hand still clutched the chopsticks. A stain of blood bloomed on her chest like a voracious blossom and right at its center, standing straight up, were the handles of "Old Reliable," the bud shears. The blades were buried to their hilt in Quintana Kingsley's chest. Calista felt an overwhelming coldness, as if her body were turning to ice on this warm summer morning. But she felt her heart swell in a tumultuous thudding. Her rib cage seemed too narrow for her heart. It would burst, burst like that dark red blossom on Quintana's chest. Calista screamed and ran from the greenhouse.

# 5

There was a blank period, lost minutes, between the time she fled from the greenhouse and ran back into the Baldwins' to call the police. She could not remember exactly what she had said or done. She could not even be sure of what she had seen, the reality of it. It was as if all images and words had been erased; that sentient life had suddenly stopped; that she had entered a state of suspended animation. Had she told the police to come to the Baldwins' or the Kingsleys'? Where was she standing when they arrived in their screaming cars, the sirens splitting the shady green calm of the square. The double-parked cars with the flashing lights looked odd on the street with the handsome redbrick Greek Revival row houses facing the meticulously kept enclosed rectangular green.

"You mean I have to go back in there?" she heard herself saying to a policeman.

"Yes, deah." It was the Irish *dear* of an old rheumy-eyed Irish cop. "Don't worry, there are lots of people in there now. You won't be alone, deah. We'll all be there to help you."

"Help me do what?" Calista said. Just what was expected of her? The radios from the patrol cars were blaring. The cop walked over a few feet to it and reached inside. "Five-three here, Jimmy, confirmed homicide. Go ahead."

"Eight-two, detectives have responded," a voice crackled back.

An officer came out the front door of the house. He wiped his brow. "Day like this, we're going to need some floaters.

"Ma'am, will you just follow me in. And please remember when we get inside, it's very important not to touch anything."

Two more cars pulled up. A woman in a beige pleated skirt got out from the driver's side. From the other side, a man stepped out into the street. Neither one was in uniform. The woman carried a large black satchel.

"Hi, Donna."

She ran her fingers through her dark hair and pulled off her sunglasses. "We need masks yet?"

"Not yet, but soon on a day like this."

"Don't tell me about it. I'm supposed to be at the beach with my two kids."

"Al sick?" the first, older cop asked.

"Well, he better not be at the beach!" They all laughed. "Let's go." She nodded at the two officers and Calista. Calista's feet moved, although her mind seemed to remain somewhere out on the sidewalk. But she flowed along with the others on a current of small talk.

"Nice house."

"Most of these are condos now . . . just a few single owners, I'd imagine."

"Taxes'll kill you on something like this."

"Apparently, it wasn't taxes, however." Donna tossed a laugh over her shoulder, then looked up at a rather severe portrait on the wall. "Who's that?"

"Cotton Mather," Calista offered. Oh man, she thought, count on me. A veritable fount of useless information. Anyone want to play Trivial Pursuit at the scene of the crime? Calista Jacobs can be your genial host. But it was a rather good portrait of a rather bad man. Calista had been curious about the picture the first time she saw it and Quintana had said that indeed both the Kingsleys and her family, the Parkingtons, were descendants of the grim Puritan preacher.

They were making their way through the maze of pantries and back halls off the kitchen. Suddenly, Calista stopped. She could not move. She turned her head. A drawing on the wall stared at her with its saucer eyes and lopped-off hands. She thought of those shears plunged into Quintana's chest, the blossom of red blood swelling on her breast.

"Something the matter?" someone said to her. Everything! What a stupid question. She swallowed and looked at them. They were all looking at her with great expectation. She licked her lips and scratched her head. "Look." She inhaled sharply. "I don't know whether I can do this. I don't know what you want me to do." Donna had walked on. All business, that woman. "I know this is old hat to you. I read the papers. I know this is the— what?—the one hundred and twentieth murder in Boston this year, but for me . . ." Calista's voice trailed off.

"It's okay," said Jack, the older cop. Then the other officer and the man who had accompanied Donna plunged in with all the robust charm of cheerleaders at a pep rally.

"Don't worry."

"You'll do fine. Just don't touch anything."

"Yeah, don't touch. That's important until the Crime Scene Unit gets here."

"It won't take long. You'll be terrific."

They were better than cheerleaders; they were like your best buddies at camp telling you that yes, you could dive off the high board. There was nothing to it. Then someone said something about a witness.

"Me? Why?" Calista asked.

"Well, you discovered the body."

* * *

And before she knew it, she was moving along, out the scullery, through the potting shed, and into the greenhouse. Quintana was still there. Kneeling beside her, Donna had one hand jammed in her skirt pocket and with the other she held a small rectangular box into which she was mumbling. The man who had come with her was moving around the greenhouse, also mumbling into a small box. Another squad car had evidently arrived with one uniformed cop and two plainclothesmen. The greenhouse seemed ready to burst.

"So what have we got?"

"One white female, late seventies." So this is what it all comes down to, Calista thought.

"Donna," one of them said, "do me a favor. Let's not move her yet."

"Okay by me. Did you bring your mask? It's hot today."

"Any witnesses?"

"One."

The man turned immediately to Calista. "I'm Detective Brant. Can you tell me what you know?"

"I came here . . . well, I don't know what time it was, maybe nine o'clock, to sketch here in Mrs. Kingsley's greenhouse. I . . . I was drawing pictures, making studies of her plants . . . these bonsai plants. She was an expert in their cultivation."

"Hurh." The detective made a low grunting sound that Calista supposed was to indicate some mild curiosity. Although it was hard to imagine bonsai was a consuming interest of this man. Flashbulbs started to pop; another man was laying out a tape measure and another chalking the brick floor. Calista watched as he drew a chalk circle around the smashed juniper, the needles of which rested in a pool of blood.

*A lover's pinch was death.* The words seemed to pop from nowhere into her head. Who said that? Calista wondered. What dumb fool had written that nonsense? "The stroke of death is as a lover's pinch, which hurts, and is desired." Calista could not take her eyes off the shears sticking straight out of the chest. Some lover's pinch! Shakespeare . . . that was the fool. *Antony and Cleopatra*. Something about "thou and nature can so gently part." Calista looked at the smashed juniper. Eighty years, it had lasted—the two of them had lasted—and now this.

"Ms. Jacobs?"

"Oh, I'm sorry. I was distracted."

"It's understandable."

"By the way, she is not late seventies. She's eighty. Same age as the plant on the floor." At that moment, everyone paused in their little ministrations and looked at Calista, then resumed their work.

"Did you use the phone from here when you reported the body?" the detective asked.

"No, no, I ran back to the house where I'm staying."

"Good."

Why would that be good? Calista wondered. Her question was soon answered. "Would there be any prints of yours around here?"

"Why yes. On those." She pointed toward the shears protruding from Quintana's chest.

"The scissors?" Nobody missed a beat, but Calista was rather overwhelmed by what she had just said. "Well, yes. I was here yesterday and Quintana—Mrs. Kingsley asked me to hand them to her."

Donna was now lifting the hand and putting each finger over a small bowl, then scraping underneath the nails. Calista watched. At some imperceptible moment, the body had ceased to be a person. It was now an object. A name seemed superfluous, almost ridiculous. She had to stifle a giggle. She remembered suddenly that when Charley was seven or eight, he'd had a wart removed. The doctor had let him keep it in a little bottle of preservative and Charley had named it Freddy. She was trying to stifle the giggle, but then suddenly there was a tincture in the air. Someone slammed a mask under her chin, but it couldn't catch it all. She was throwing up. The sour-sweet stink in the air was roiling in her sinuses.

"It's okay. Happens all the time." They were all busy getting their masks on.

"I don't think we need her here anymore."

"Okay, I'll take you home," the old cop said with that wonderful lilt in his voice.

As she began to walk from the greenhouse, she saw them affixing a tag to the left big toe. Tag 'em and bag 'em. Or, as Henry James was reputed to have said of his impending death, "So here it is at last, the distinguished thing!" No slouch when it came to irony, that man.

6

Calista had a tremendous urge to go home and get clean, or get clean and then go home, home to Cambridge. For if she recalled correctly, this week all the water was turned off in her house while they were redoing the piping—five thousand dollars' worth of copper piping. All the perks of the Louisburg Square house that she had so frequently calculated had suddenly evaporated. She was left with fear and this dreadful stench still hovering deep in her sinuses. She stood in the shower and scrubbed furiously. She wished she had brought the Dr. Bonner's peppermint soap, or was it eucalyptus? Whatever it was, it was strong. If anything could chase away that horrific sweet-sour stench, it would be Dr. Bonner's. She felt the bile rising in the back of her throat again. She squeezed her eyes shut and bit her lip while the hot water beat down on her head. She rode it out. The wave of nausea passed. She got out of the shower and toweled off.

She put on her robe, sat in a chair by the window, and propped her feet up. A crowd had begun to gather. Neighbors from the other houses around the square were milling on the sidewalk.

Some of the police were leaving. The body had evidently been removed. Oh dear! She saw a young cop bending over an open hydrant. He was washing out something. She knew what. It was his mask, which she had thrown up into. Her vomit flowing down the gutters of the elegant streets of Louisburg Square. There goes the neighborhood!

She had to get her wits together. First things first. She must go over to the Public Garden and tell Charley. Then she had to go over to Cambridge and see just how livable their house was. Certainly they should be able to camp out in some fashion. But what about the cats? The fucking cats. Did she have to take them to Cambridge, too? No, that's why they weren't in Maine. Traveling, changes exacerbated their conditions. Too unsettling, that's what Nan had said. Cambridge seemed as far away as Maine at this moment; the Charles River as definitive as the Rubicon. So that meant no for Nestor and Ophelia. Calista would come back to feed them and let them out for romps in the garden, but she'd be damned if she were going to schlepp Piss and Moan to Cambridge. She was sure her house would be very upsetting to them. It would deliver the coup de grâce to Ophelia's bladder and Nestor's psyche. Not that she cared, but it would not endear her to Nan and Will, for whom she did care a great deal.

As she walked down Charles Street toward the gardens, she wondered exactly how she would tell Charley this. Not that he even knew Quintana Kingsley. Maybe he had met her once. This was the height of the tourist season in Boston. The swan boats were loaded with good folks from Iowa or Washington State or wherever, drinking in American history and doing quaint things like riding the swan boats. Calista tried to picture herself telling Charley. Most likely at this very moment, he was sitting between the immense wings of the boat and pedaling benchloads of passengers. Didn't seem quite kosher to break the news in such idyllic surroundings.

When she arrived at the duck pond, the line for the swan boats seemed half a mile long. Charley was not on line patrol, nor was he at the ticket booth. As far as she could tell, he was not on the float, either, guiding people onto the boats. This meant he was on the high "mimic sea," a poetic name sometimes given the kidney-shaped pond. Matthew, Charley's friend from Cambridge, spotted her as she approached the ticket booth. He, too, was working on the swan boats this summer.

"Hi, Cal. Charley's out. He's coming under the bridge now."

"Do you think he can take a break? I gotta talk to him."

"Nope. We're really shorthanded this week. Can you talk to him on the boat?"

She hesitated. Beside her, she could hear a family having an argument about whether to finish the Freedom Trail before or after lunch. They all looked hot and tired and very aggravated with one another. Typical family vacation. What would she be ruining with a little talk of murder? She'd keep her voice low. "Sure," she said quickly to Matthew. "Can you get me on?"

"Yep."

"Let her through," he said to the man at the turnstile. "This is Charley's mom. She needs to talk to him."

Five minutes later, Calista, her hand gripping the scalloped edge of the swan's fiberglass wing, stood next to Charley. He pedaled steadily toward the northwest corner of the pond.

"You actually threw up?"

"Charley, I don't even want to talk about it. The very thought of that smell." She began to taste it again in the back of her throat. And she could hardly claim seasickness on a swan boat.

"Well, who'd want to kill that old lady?" A man with a baby on his lap on the bench directly in front of Charley turned around. He wore a Miami Dolphins T-shirt and had a very sunburned nose.

"Not so loud, Charley?" She bent over and whispered the words in his ear. "So listen, can you get off early?"

"No way, José. They need all the help they can get here. They've got two people out this week. And the crowds are brutal."

"Oh gosh, that reminds me. Mrs. Kingsley asked me if I could ask you about a job for her grandson. I didn't give her much hope." It sounded strange to talk about hope now.

"They'd hire him in a minute this week."

"Well, I doubt if he'd be in much shape after all this to pedal a swan boat."

"They'd hire a quadriplegic with a strong tongue today."

"Oh, Charley!" Calista couldn't help but laugh. She might as well settle back and enjoy the rest of the ride. They were just going under the bridge now and would round the rock island at the east end of the pond, where the baby ducks floated like little fluff balls behind their mother. Boy oh boy! she thought. Robert McCloskey had really hit it when he came up with the idea of *Make Way for Ducklings.* People from all corners of the earth came now to these gardens because of that gentle old man and his wonderful drawings. He had done the very finest thing an artist can do—make a real place live in the imagination forever. That is genius, she thought. So many of the new illustrators were into a high-gloss slick illustration, dazzling in technique but yielding drawings that were so airless, they seemed literally to gasp for life. Somewhat the opposite was the retro fine arts trend, with illustrators intent on painting in a grand European tradition. But those drawings, too, lacked, if not life, soul. They seemed rather characterless. In either case, none of these illustrators could hold a candle to McCloskey or Sendak. Not one had any sense of how to really draw. They were great technicians, but most significantly they had no sense of narrative.

The boat pulled up to the float. Calista got out. It was settled. She would pack up a few things for Charley and herself and they would meet back in Cambridge and see whether their house was remotely livable.

"Are you sure you don't want to take the cats, Mom?" Charley said as she disembarked.

"I am sure."

"Do you think they'll be okay?"

"They'll be fine. I'll go over every day and check on them. I just don't want them in Cambridge. I don't need those cats in Cambridge. Those cats have an attitude."

"Mom, that's the whole point of being a cat—having an attitude."

Calista looked at her son. He actually wore a little captain's hat to command this vessel and his fiery red hair stood out shaggy around his ears. A shadow from its bill sliced across the top part of his face so she couldn't see the lucid gray eyes. He had, of course, uttered one of the profound truths of the world. And with such ease, with such grace, he wore this mantle of wisdom. She wondered suddenly whether there were some great rabbis among their ancestors. It would seem that this kind of insight coupled with the grace, the very posture, must be genetic. It must come out of some august tradition of looking into the souls of things.

But as far as she knew, there was only one great "rabbi" in their past, their most recent past, and that was Charley's father, Tom Jacobs. *Rabbi,* after all, meant teacher, and Tom had looked into the soul of the universe. For he had probed the very beginnings of the universe, the beginnings of time. His area of expertise had been those first slivers of the first second after the big bang. And his major concern: When did time begin? Tom would often quote St. Augustine to his students: When asked what did God do before there was a universe created by Him, Augustine replied that time was a property of the universe God created and that time did not exist before the beginning of the universe. That, of course, was why the Pope was crazy about Tom—because Tom was the most eloquent proponent and explicator of the big bang theory and the big bang came the closest to Genesis and allowed for at least a cameo appearance by God.

The Vatican had had a conference on cosmology that Tom and Calista had attended. That was when the Pope had taken such a shine, as it 'twere, to Tom's ideas. Calista had loved Tom for other reasons. And now as she walked back to 16 Louisburg Square, she began to miss him just horribly. She missed Archie, too. But right now, she missed Tom more. It had been almost five years since his death, his murder in the desert. She would never get over it. She would always love him. She would always love Archie. Loving two men forever was not hard. Missing two men and knowing you would have to go on missing one forever was very hard.

Waves of heat shimmered up from the brick sidewalk as she turned onto Mt. Vernon from Charles Street and began the steep climb up Beacon Hill toward the cool green oasis of Louisburg Square. Its coolness as well as its tranquillity were perhaps just a mirage. Perhaps the lives of entire families that lived behind the elegant Georgian facades were nothing more than mirages.

# 7

As Calista stood in the alcove where her bed was and looked straight up at the sky through a hole in the roof that a baby elephant might fit, she did wonder what it was that had ever given her the notion she could manage even to camp in this house.

"Well, I think it might be okay for tonight. We can sheet that with some plastic, take the drop cloth off your bed. I mean, the weather's supposed to be good. No rain predicted." Michael Stephanotis laughed. "No shower, either!" he said, nodding toward the bathroom.

"You mean the water's not hooked up yet? I thought that was supposed to happen today."

"Well, they ran out of bends for the piping and Peter had to go out to Braintree to pick some stuff up. So he should have them tomorrow. And you know how Peter drives."

"I know. I worry about plumbers who drive Porsches and wear Armani suits."

"Mom!" Charley said in a genuinely shocked voice.

"I know, I know. I'm not politically correct. It's very hard to be when I'm dirty and tired and want my house back."

She sighed and looked around. There was plaster dust over everything. God forbid she should have a headache and want an aspirin. Nothing was where it should be. She had packed all the contents of the bathroom up in boxes because they were having to tear into walls behind cabinets to get into the piping. And then to save her clothes and books from dust, they had all been packed up and moved to a back room or the basement. But what else could she do? She might as well try it for a night. Maybe Michael's guys could move the television and VCR upstairs for her. Part of her intended therapy involved watching *Singin' in the Rain* and having a tot of Mount Gay rum—all in bed. A kind of two-step recovery program from murder.

Gene Kelly had been her first serious movie-star crush after Roy Rogers, who didn't count because he was strictly prelatency. No, Gene was genuinely sexy. She, of course, loved Fred Astaire for his nearly ethereal elegance, but Gene had that low center of gravity that gave him a very earthy grace. And his wit. The part in the rain number where he did the shuffle crossovers up and down into the wet gutter drove Calista crazy. And then there was Donald O'Connor's showstopping "Make 'Em Laugh." Talk about funny. No, she would definitely stay for a couple of nights. She could always go back to number 16 to shower. She had to look in on the cats, anyway. And maybe for the weekend, she'd go up to Vermont. But she'd better call Lieutenant O'Leary and tell him where she was. He had said to keep in touch. So had Detective Brant.

"They want to see me? The kids? . . . Yes, yes. I guess so. Well, tomorrow. I'm pretty tired now. Thank you for telling them that. Yes. . . . Okay, good-bye." She hung up. "Oh shit."

"What's the trouble, Mom?" Charley walked in.

"Oh, it's just that Quintana Kingsley's children and I guess her brother want to talk to me . . . you know, seeing as I was the one to discover her."

"Oh jeez." Charley sighed and leaned against the doorjamb. A shower of plaster dust sprinkled down into his hair.

"Well, I can understand it. It's just that it's not going to be exactly pleasant, and it looks as if I'm going to have to go to the funeral, too. It's Saturday," she said with a sour look.

"You were thinking about Vermont for this weekend?"

"Precisely."

Too bad the Kingsleys weren't Jewish, Calista thought wistfully. They'd never be buried on a Saturday.

She had been asleep for hours before she felt it: wet and cold right on her nose. She opened her eyes and stared up. Then she heard the unmistakable sound. Another drop, then another on her forehead. Slowly, the knowledge dawned. I am not singing in the rain. "Shit!" She sat straight up in bed. A rivulet of water from a crease in the plastic began to funnel down on her sheets. "I don't believe this," Calista muttered in the dark. She stood up to examine where Michael had tacked the plastic, but the rain was coming down harder. All she could say was "shit" and all she could think was that there was a literary term for this. It was either objective correlative or pathetic fallacy, but one minute you're watching *Singing in the Rain* and the next minute you're being drenched in bed. That was the gist of it.

It was hopeless. She got up, spread the drop cloth over the bed, took her comforter, and threw it down with her pillow on the floor in Charley's bedroom, which was also a mess but didn't have a hole in the roof.

# 8

Calista was watching Bootsie carefully as she spoke. Her head seemed to bend with the completion of each piece of information, each thought, as if this nodding was somehow helping her to digest it. It seemed to Calista that Bootsie was summoning all of her intellectual strength just to concentrate on the words. It was amply clear to Calista that Bootsie had been drinking steadily, probably since she first heard the news. A bemused look sometimes seemed to drift through the elongated celadon eyes. There was a large tumbler with gin or vodka that Bootsie rested her hand on lightly. She had been nursing it for a long time. It had not gone down that much since Calista had come over.

"See, Bootsie, did you hear what Calista just said? What the police told her—same as what they said to us." Gus Kingsley, Bootsie's older brother, leaned forward and touched her knee lightly with his hand in a tender gesture. Bootsie looked down at the hand that rested for just a second on her knee. Her face darkened and for the first time her glaze seemed to begin to crack. But then she looked up and stared through her brother. "Yes, I heard. Mummy didn't suffer much because the shears cut right through the aorta." Very slowly she turned her head toward Calista. "Comforting, isn't it?" There was a look of pure venom in her eyes.

Calista sat in the living room of Bootsie's large house in the Cottage Farm area of Brookline, Boston's first suburb. For those who wanted to be near the city but in a good public school system, Brookline was a premiere choice. Rambling old stucco and brick houses were set on large plots of land with big trees. Close to the great hospitals of Boston, it was popular with doctors. It had a large Jewish population now, but still the old WASPs, the ones who couldn't quite go the distance to the North Shore or pay the taxes on Beacon Hill, found a tranquil refuge here. Bootsie was one.

After her divorce, she had decided Brookline was just the place for her and Jamie. Of course, the family had a fit when she said he would attend public school and they insisted that he continue at Poulton Academy, where all Kingsley men had gone since it opened over one hundred years before. It was unthinkable for a Kingsley not to go to Poulton, which was dedicated to high thinking and plain living. It was the place where scions of cold roast Boston could meet, where bonds that would influence their business, intellectual, and social lives would be forged. The Kingsleys were unswerving in their devotion to Poulton Academy. They would no more think of not sending a son to Old Pulley, as it was called, than give up their pew in King's Chapel, their membership to The Country Club, or, horror of horrors, not go to Harvard.

In fact, the Kingsleys felt that the Baldwins were positively bohemian for having never done more than a few of those very things. Will Baldwin himself had attended Poulton but had been thrown out in 1922 for mooning a teacher. Needless to say, he was not keen on having his son Archie go there. And although Will had gone on to Harvard, Archie had elected to go to Dartmouth. The whole lot of Baldwins were a bunch of agnostics, so King's Chapel had been out of the question for years. Finally, nobody played golf, so why belong to something like the Country Club?

Poor Bootsie, Calista thought as she looked around the spare but nicely furnished living room. She had tried so hard to escape all that. It was apparent from the Mies Van der Rohe chair to the glass coffee tables and stark white walls. There was an airiness to the room. Things had been peeled back to show the elegant moldings, the nicely curved double bay in the front of the living room. There were a few Oriental rugs and some truly spectacular Asian pieces, including four beautiful ink-wash Japanese scrolls from the Edo period. One depicted cranes in flight over a waterfall and another showed a mountain shrouded in clouds. These scrolls and a massive chandelier of the late Victorian period were Bootsie's major concessions to an older tradition in terms of style, along with a wing chair in which she sat now, her jaw tilted up, her head back. She held the scrolls in her gaze through half-closed eyes as she twirled the ice in her drink with her index finger. Gus stood behind her, resting his hand on her shoulder.

"Boots . . . Boots . . ." Gus spoke softly, patting her lightly on her shoulder. "Are you going to be okay?"

"Yes, yes, of course."

"Should I call Dr. Miles?"

"No, no . . . that's not necessary. Jamie . . ." She coughed nervously. A pained look crossed her face. She lowered her voice and muttered, "Jamie will be here. He'll take care of me."

"Yes, I guess so." Gus rose quickly. "Well, I better be going. Uncle Rudy's flight is due in soon. I'll just drive him directly to the Harvard Club. Then I'm afraid I have to go out to St. Bennett's. You know I always coach tennis on Tuesdays and Thursdays, and what with playoffs on the day when the funeral is scheduled, I better make some arrangements for the team." Gus was scratching his head and speaking to no one in particular. "Yes, I have to show Murphy the lineup for the playoffs, since I won't be there and . . ." Gus's voice dwindled off.

"You go and get Rudy. Then go out to St. Bennett's. That'll be fine," Bootsie said mechanically, and reached for her drink. She took a big swallow. Gus's eyebrows knitted together in a worried look. He gestured with his head to Calista as if he wanted to speak to her alone.

"Well, I better be on my way, too," Calista said, and jumped up. "I . . ." she hesitated. It sounded so dumb. "I hope that I've been of some help. I'm just so sorry that . . ." her voice faded. There was nothing she could say, absolutely nothing. Oh yes, she could tell them that she had been in the same place almost five years before when Tom was murdered, but what good would that do? Nothing, simply nothing at all.

Bootsie mumbled something as Calista left and seemed to try to wave good-bye with her thin white hand. It looked so delicate, that hand, like a brushstroke from one of the Chinese artist's scrolls. And then once more she remembered the strange children's drawings in the back hall off the pantries of 18 Louisburg Square. Suddenly, she wondered what had happened to the other Kingsley daughter. She remembered now that Bootsie had said some of the drawings had been done by her sister. No one had mentioned a sister at all since the murder. Surely if she was alive, she would have been one of the "kids" that had wanted to speak to Calista. Gus was now motioning to her.

"Obviously, we've got a little problem here with Bootsie." His voice was a husky whisper as he bent his head down to speak closely to Calista. Gus Kingsley was a tall man, early fifties, with a gangly kind of grace. "Well, it's not your problem," he quickly amended. "It's just that as you might have guessed, she has a problem with alcohol. It understandably gets worse under stress like this. She's a binger." He paused. "I was a quiet but steady drunk myself." Calista's eyes widened at this sudden admission. "I'm a recovering alcoholic," he said simply. And then Calista's question was answered. "Muffy, our other sister, died of it."

"Has Bootsie made any attempts to recover?"

"Not really. You see, in a sense she was never as . . ." He stopped and searched for a word. "As obviously impaired as we were. And quite frankly, she didn't drink as much. But lately, Mother and I both noticed it's been getting worse. And we're worried about all the pills she takes."

"What kind of pills?"

"Well, she does have some sort of thyroid condition. So she takes something for that. She claims that the doctor said she could drink with these . . . but I'm not sure if that's exactly the truth. Or maybe the doctor doesn't know quite how much she drinks. And then she's always had insomnia problems. And Jamie's a real handful lately. So she's been a nervous wreck over him. She mentioned that the doctor gave her something to calm her nerves."

"Oh God." Calista sighed.

"Yeah, right," Gus said in a tired voice. She looked at him. He had very tired, shadowed eyes. They were almost unreadable. But she liked him. He had a simplicity about him, a directness. He seemed terribly concerned about Bootsie. "Well, I must run. Pick up Uncle Rudy. You'll see him at the funeral. He's quite bizarre!"

"Oh!" Well, maybe there will be something to look forward to at the funeral, after all, Calista thought.

Just then, a young boy about Charley's age came bounding up the steps. "Jamie!" Gus said, his face brightening. But Jamie whizzed right by his uncle. "Might you at least say hello to Calista Jacobs here, the woman who discovered Grandma?"

"Hello," he said without turning his head. It was as spectacular a display of rudeness as only a profoundly angry adolescent could muster.

## 9

Calista stood nervously on the corner of Park and Tremont. She was scanning the people drifting along the paths that cut diagonally across the Common in the rising heat of the morning. No sign of Charley. She felt stupid standing there with his sports jacket, shirt, and tie on a hanger. Just where did he plan to change? A phone booth? It hadn't been her idea that he come to the funeral. He had volunteered, managed to find someone to fill in for him at the swan boats and would work a double-duty lunch break in return. Where there was a will, there was a way—and Charley wanted to go to the funeral, "scope it out," as he put it. She knew why. It was a challenge in the same way the electronic mazes of the computer challenged him. There was a code to be broken, passwords to be generated, access systems to be cracked. Suddenly, she saw him walking toward her. He certainly did not have the mien of one going to a funeral. He bounced along with an easy gait that defied both the rising heat and the occasion.

"Howdy doo, Tiggy-Mom."

"Try to restrain your ebullience, Charley."

"You look so Mrs. Tiggy-Winkle-ish—your hair is really out there."

"I know. It's the humidity." She handed him the hanger with the jacket and shirt, then touched the mass of silvery hair that foamed around her head. She tried to reanchor some of it with her industrial-strength barrettes. "Listen," she said, a bobby pin in her mouth, "where are you planning on changing for this event?"

"No problem." He took the shirt off the hanger, handed the rest back to her, and proceeded to slip it over his swan boat T-shirt. Within fifty feet of King's Chapel, he was knotting his tie. As they started up the steps, he put on the jacket. Calista had chucked the hanger into a trash can. They joined a throng of somber people. Under their summer tans, they all wore a strained look—not so much out of sorrow as from being called back to Boston from summer homes on the Cape, the Vineyard, Manchester-by-the-Sea, the coast of Maine, camps on tranquil golden lakes in New Hampshire or Canada for this tragic, yes, but ultimately confusing end to a life properly led. Indeed, Quintana Kingsley could have avoided all of this if she had gone up to Nohqwha, the family's lake retreat in New Hampshire. But alas, their house up there had been undergoing major reconstruction and was not ready. Perhaps it couldn't have been avoided even if she had gone away. There was no forced entry into the house. Nothing had been stolen. It looked for all intents and purposes as if Quintana might have known her murderer. So he or she could have achieved their goal at Nohqwha as well as at Louisburg Square.

Calista and Charley slipped into a boxed pew. There was a handsome family that looked as if it had just changed out of tennis gear across from her. Calista had forgotten this quaint detail of the first Church of England in the Massachusetts Bay Colony—the occupants of these boxed pews must sit facing one another. It was slightly unsettling given the occasion.

The rector began. A simple prayer from the Book of Common Prayer, as simple and spare as the clean lines of a dory. No room for ambiguity; perhaps that was the whole point. It was a prayer about accepting the blessings of life with grace and basically shutting up about the mysterious ways in which God works; plain New England homespun. No kvetching here. Shut up: That set the tone for the rest of the service. These people didn't know what they were missing by not being Jewish, Calista thought. She looked over at Charley. He was discreetly scanning the mourners. They all sat behind stony faces. Occasionally, an eye brimmed; there might be a sniffle or two. That was all. Calista spotted Bootsie. She sat in a pew just under a north window. Although deathly pale, she possessed a radiance; she seemed created out of nuances of light and shadow that at certain angles became dazzling. As Calista looked at Bootsie, it struck her that she seemed not quite real, but indeed like a creation of fluid brushstrokes. She could have been a portrait by John Singer Sargent. She had that ethereal yet slightly agitated quality that one associated with his women subjects: light dancing on surface, a high-strung nervous energy. It had once been said that Sargent's women were "the product of an age of nerves." That had been an era when nerves, and high-strung tension, had been elevated to a near art form. It had been just before the suffrage movement got under way, a little before Elizabeth Cady Stanton. There had been nothing but nerves for these women. They had done it well, with great style and grace; it had not been kvetching.

Even from a distance, Bootsie's eyes were remarkable, great enormous pastel smears amongst the light and shadows of her face. She stood between her son and a very elderly man. Next to the man was Gus. One could pick out the Kingsleys. There was a strong family resemblance that ran through, indicated by wide-set eyes in faces that often seemed a tad small. Kingsleys also favored high foreheads and rounded chins, with a somewhat pinched look about their noses. Of course, who knew whether the look was Kingsley or Parkington, Quintana's family. It was hard to sort these features out.

But who were all of these people at the hub of the hub, any-way? It was Oliver Wendell Holmes who had declared back in

1858 that the Boston State House was the Hub of the solar system. The name had stuck. Boston was, most Bostonians thought, the most civilized city in the world, and these people gathered in the chapel where George Washington had worshiped, with a bell made by Paul Revere, were the most civilized of the civilized. The pews were spiked with Saltonstalls, Welds, Cabots, Lodges, Forbes, and Perkins—and Baldwins. Not Nan and Will, but Calista thought she had spotted a cousin of Will's. There was a whiff to all of them—many looked overbred and underfed. The middle-aged matrons wore their darker summer wear from Talbots and some carried their Nantucket lightship wicker pocketbooks with the scrimshaw medallions on their covers. The older ones stood erect in sagging suits excavated from dry-cleaning bags, most likely Falk's, a Brookline cleaner favored by old families. Nan Baldwin had told her that once upon a time when you took your clothes to Falk's, they came back wrapped in thin paper with a tag that read: "If you send your clothes to Falk's, you can be sure these clothes will not hang next to someone's whose acquaintance you would not want to make."

There was most certainly an elitism, but that could not explain it all in Boston, the Hub. It was an elitism that had grown out of privilege. There was a difference, however: The privilege was not to be enjoyed for its own pleasure. Rather, with it there was a concomitant tradition of responsibility. If a person was born into one of the first families of Boston, that person was obligated to set a tone; there had to be certain standards, and these standards involved realizing your duty toward others. It was a sense of stewardship that came with the facts of privileged birth. Calista had no idea whether such values still persisted in many members of the Kingsley family, or other's families, for that matter. Blood had thinned out often along with brains and money over the generations. However, that sense of stewardship and responsibility was definitely alive and well in Nan and Will Baldwin and their son Archie and his siblings. They had the imagination to branch out, to see a broader world. But in many ways, the narrow world of Boston was still a very tight one, and Calista wondered whether indeed the Hub moved in relation to anything else.

The service was mercifully short. Quintana's life was not one that lent itself to elaboration or embellishment. She was not a Harriet Hemenway or a Minna Hall, pioneers in the turn-of-the-century environmental and suffrage movements and founders of the Audubon Society. And she certainly did not have the style and the money of a Mrs. Jack Gardner. Her life had revolved around the Chilton Club, the Friday-afternoon symphony, the Horticulture Society, and the annual Ellis Antiques Show.

The most colorful flourish of the funeral was an arrangement on the altar of three obscure lilies and a shaft of wheat from Ikebana Unit Number 9, a Japanese flower-arranging society to which Quintana Kingsley had belonged. And there were amidst all these Brahmins two or three Oriental faces. During the eulogy, there were several references to the sea because of the Kingsley-Parkington connection with Salem and shipping. Quintana's Colonial forebears had been heavily involved with coastal trading, and the Kingsleys of that generation had started out in the Derby wharf countinghouses of Salem and then went on to own clippers that sailed to Canton in the China Trade. Thus, the rector concluded his eulogy on the long, privileged, but simple life of Quintana Kingsley with a quote from an Emily Dickinson poem: "Exaltation is the going of an inland soul to sea . . ."

Calista loved this poem. Would those words not give some comfort to any grieving relative? She looked over toward Bootsie. Bootsie was no longer a composition of light and shadow. Her face had hardened into a venomous mask, rigid and taut, ready to crack not from grief but hatred. Calista inhaled sharply. It was a shocking face.

# 10

It was announced at the end of the service that guests were invited back to the home of the deceased's brother Diggory Parkington on Marlborough Street. "Let's go," Charley whispered.

"Well, I think I should, but really, Charley, I don't want you getting fired."

"Don't worry. I'll only stay for a little bit."

It was a venerable old building, a stone's throw from the Public Garden and one of the few on the entire street not condo-ized or owned by a college or some other institution. Built of gray stone, tall and narrow, with the stern rectitude of a Calvinist minister, the austerity of the exterior gave way to the something else almost immediately. As soon as a person stepped through the door into an octagonal foyer, one was ambushed by portraits of Italian cherubs in oval recessions in the walls. Of course, thought Calista as a uniformed maid directed her to a powder room on the second floor, the house was probably bought and decorated during the time of Mrs. Jack Gardner, who had built an Italian villa in the Fenway to house her haul of art acquired from Europe under the exquisite connoisseurship of Berenson. But it was Calista's guess that the Parkingtons not only lacked the style but the nerve of Mrs. Jack. There was immediately detectable a slight disharmony in terms of proportion and aesthetics. This was confirmed as she waited outside the powder room in a small drawing room on the second floor. There were several bucolic court paintings of the Watteau school juxtaposed with Oriental embroideries and geegaws from the China Trade. The woman who had sat across from her in the pew came out of the powder room and gave her a terse nod and a smile that could possibly have been measured in millimeters. Calista was set to give her a very warm hello. After all, they had shared the pew on an occasion that should have lent itself toward something a bit more congenial in terms of a greeting. Boxed in at King's Chapel in that sort of intimacy, even if formal and imposed, should count for something. Well, forget it.

Calista went into the powder room and tried to do something with her hair. All these WASPs with their straight hair like shining helmets on their well-shaped heads, and here she was with this froth of gray—no, silver; Archie said it was silver. She took out her pocket-sized can of hair spray—hair Mace she called it, for it was more of an act of subjugation than coiffing. In two minutes, the enemy was contained in a fairly attractive nimbus of silvery curls piled atop her head, with a few discreet tendrils falling around the edges. She took a pee, washed her hands, and went downstairs.

Diggory Parkington, a frail-looking man the color of parchment paper, was greeting guests while leaning on a walker. A nurse stood at his side. There was really no way to avoid him, but Calista worried exactly how she would explain herself. Would the knowledge that she indeed had been the one to discover the body be too much for the old soul, who looked ready to blow away with the first riffle of a wind?

"And who might you be?" He leaned forward. His bald skull had an intaglio of blue veins and Calista could imagine an aneuryism blowing up in front of her very eyes.

"Calista Jacobs, just a friend of Quintana's through gardening—Japanese gardening."

"Oh, an Ikebana gal!" He shook her hand warmly; a gracious smile, and then she moved on.

As she walked through a front parlor into the living room, she spotted Charley talking with Jamie McPhee by a table with platters of food. She scanned the room for Bootsie and spotted her, drink in hand, talking animatedly to a middle-aged man. She seemed propped up by the sheer animation of her talk. Her hands flew in antic gestures. A coquettish rictus twitched across her face. She would turn her shoulders this way and that in a constant series of minute adjustments, almost like a fashion model trying to arrange herself in the camera's lens. But it was all a jangle of nerves masked by poses and chatter and gesture.

"Here, how about a drink?" Calista felt a light touch on her elbow. It was Gus Kingsley. "The last thing she needs," he said, nodding toward his sister. "This is Pimm's with a slice of cucumber. It can be quite restorative on a day like this."

"Oh, thank you, thank you so much. Has she really been drinking all morning?"

"Actually, I don't think so. It might very possibly be the pills."

"This all sounds terribly dangerous. Have you talked to her doctor?"

"Oh yes. Everyone has talked to her doctor. And he has tried to wean her from the pills. But she still finds ways of getting them, and she is not inclined to do anything about the drinking. It's just a really difficult situation and it's not doing any good for Jamie. I just met your son, by the way—Charley. They are over there talking together. Very nice young fellow."

"Oh, thank you. You know your mother had asked if maybe Charley could get Jamie a job on the swan boats—that's where he's working this summer."

"Oh, that would be terrific. . . ." Gus's face brightened.

"Gussy!" Two long, elegant, and tanned arms snaked around Gus's middle.

"Bambi, dear."

I don't believe these names, Calista thought. She turned. Bambi was none other than her pew mate. Great. Oh well, no WASP princess called Bambi was going to undo her. Calista extended her hand immediately before Gus had a chance to introduce her. "Calista Jacobs." Then she turned to Gus. "We shared a pew." No getting out of it, cutie pie.

Bambi's mouth opened partway, just to that point on Calista's oven called "the broil position"—for the door when you want to run convection.

"You're not the one who does the children's books, are you . . . that Calista Jacobs?"

"Yes."

"Oh my Gawd! I don't believe it. Wait till I find Maisie and Tigger. You are their absolute favorite."

Great. So now you can smile at me and act civil instead of like upstairs, where it looked as if you thought that I might pee on your head instead of in the toilet. Calista assumed that Maisie and Tigger were children and not pets. "And you're Archie Baldwin's friend, aren't you?"

"Yes."

"Oh Gawd, he is so handsome." She ran her long fingers up across her forehead in one of those calculated gestures that people of little substance often use to punctuate their conversations. "He's older than I am, of course, but we all had crushes on him— you know, back then, Waltz Evenings and deb parties."

"Archie never cottoned to that sort of thing, as I recall," said Gus. "Never went to many, unless he was roped in to it."

"Yes, I would imagine that would be true. It fits," Calista said.

"So bright, though!" Bambi said, leaning forward. Again it was a gesture meant to convey understanding of Archie's work and career, yet it masked the fact that this woman knew absolutely nothing of what Archie did. This was, of course, the art of small talk. It let the conversation run on with no one getting into deep doo-doo.

"Where's Archie now?" Gus asked.

"Guatemala—Batan Grande, a Mayan site. . . ." She was starting to lose Bambi, she could tell.

"Listen, dear." Bambi was slipping her arm through Gus's. "I really came here on a mission: to abduct dear Gussie to come over and see Grummy in the library." She turned to Calista. "Gus has always been a favorite of Grummy's, my grandmother, and she can't walk. Grummy was Queenie's cousin. So I hope you don't mind me taking him off like this. . . ."

"Oh no, not at all."

"I'll see you, Calista," he said as Bambi led him away.

Bambi tossed a broad smile over her shoulder at Calista. "It's great meeting you. A real celebrity!"

Celebrity my foot, asshole. Calista smiled back sweetly. Just then, she remembered whom Bambi reminded her of—Jordan Baker, the athletic Long Island beauty in *The Great Gatsby* who cheated at tennis. And she bet dollars to doughnuts that Bambi was cheating at something else here. She didn't believe for one minute that bit about Grummy. Oh maybe she was in the library, but there was something about the way Bambi leaned into Gus's body that suggested the library was just an interim stop to someplace else.

Calista stood there trying to look occupied with her drink while simultaneously taking in more of the room. The room was a grand salon with marquetry parquet floors, worn Oriental rugs, twenty-foot-high ceilings, and a massive fireplace. She moved toward a long table supported by griffins on which some food had been set out. Cucumber sandwiches, brittle little crackers with some sort of repulsive-looking paste smeared on them, and a ham that had been hacked at most brutally by an inept carver. She couldn't help but recall Quintana, a mere seventy-two hours before, ministering with her delicate instruments to her ancient plants. But then her mind was flooded by the horrible image of the shears, the blossom of blood spreading on the chest. It had not been spreading, however, when she had discovered Quintana. It had already stopped. So why, Calista wondered, did her mind always see it in motion—the bloom unfolding like time-lapse photography of a blossom opening on a plant?

She took another sip of her drink and looked around some more. She was standing near a tall Palladian window with elaborate velvet drapery. In the middle of the window, there was a palm in an immense chinoiserie pot. It had a bad case of aphids or mites. She wasn't sure which. The lower fronds were desiccated and beginning to wither. As she looked down, she spotted a dead mouse nestled in the bottom of the drapery fringe that brushed the floor. To one side of the window were two hand-colored lithographs of something Egyptian. She moved closer to examine them. One was the Great Temple of Ammon in Karnak; the inscription on the other was the Grand Portico of the Temple of Isis in Philae. They were exquisite lithographs by none other than David Roberts, a nineteenth-century Scottish lithographer. Calista had studied folios of his work at the Tate in London. She would guess these to be the most valuable pieces in the house. As she gazed around the shabby splendor of the room, she realized that what she was looking at was the real thing! This, in fact, was uncorrected Ralph Lauren. Ralph reinvented the past, leaving out the dead mouse, velvet drapes worn so thin that the sunlight came through, the aphids on the palm. Lauren's vision was always more perfect than the past ever had been. Truly the pluperfect! But this untouched history, this peculiar *tableau vivant* of cold roast Boston, was terribly exotic in its own way. And what, thought Calista, was that poised in an arched doorway like some strange hothouse plant? The sight did not just catch her eye but arrested her entire attention. The man was the most peculiar-looking creature Calista had ever seen.

"Mom, I've got to go now or I'll be late. That kid Jamie is going to meet me over there later. I think they might hire him."

Charley had come up behind her and was speaking quietly in her ear, but Calista could not take her eyes off the figure in the doorway. "Charley, over there in the doorway, do you know who that man is?"

"Man?"

The figure was most definitely odd-looking and certainly seemed to fall between genders. Small, quite thin, the gentleman stood erect in an intriguingly cut suit, the jacket of which seemed midway between a Victorian frock coat and a shorter, more casual jacket. Beneath the jacket, there was a fairly sumptuous-looking waistcoat in a muted apricot color. The effect was sheer elegance. But the gentleman who wore it defied imagination. His hair was parted down the middle and obviously dyed, almost a burgundy color. His eyebrows leapt like small minnows above a pair of permanently startled-looking eyes. From Calista's vantage point, he reminded her of a deer just at the moment when it catches a whiff of the hunter. He looked about to bolt. Calista, however, hoped fervently he would not. She was inexorably drawn to him. Whoever was he? She felt a small tap on her wrist. A little voice scratched the air.

"My mom said you wrote a book we sort of like . . ." Calista looked down. There was a small boy of seven or eight. He stood waist-high and had the same golden blond hair as his mother. "She said we should come over and talk to you."

"She did, did she?" Calista replied in a distracted manner. Shit on Bambi! Just when things were getting interesting.

"Yep," said another little voice. Standing by the boy was a beautiful little girl of perhaps five.

"I've read all your books," said the little girl.

"No, you haven't, Maisie. You haven't read *The Boy Who Could Fly,* because we lost it before you were old enough for it. So just shut up." Then he turned to Calista. "Our mother said we should ask you what you are writing a book about now."

"Oh, she told you to ask that, did she?"

"Yep," both children answered.

"Well, how about you ask me a question that you want to ask and not your mom? A question of your very own."

"We don't have any," the boy said, and they both stood as still as small statues, looking up at her.

Great. How was she going to dump these kids? She really wanted to work over to the other side of the room and meet the peculiar little gentleman.

"You know," the little girl said suddenly, "you don't look nearly as old as your hair."

Calista bit her lip and suppressed a chuckle. There was hope for Maisie. "You know, dear, that's a marvelous observation. Maybe you'll grow up and be an artist someday."

"Hah!" The little boy laughed harshly.

Well, screw you, sonny, Calista thought. "But in the meantime, I see a very old lady in the corner and she looks as if she might enjoy some of those cookies they are serving. It might be nice if you took her some and a glass of tea."

"Oh, that's Grummy," Tigger was saying, "and she's half-crocked and she won't drink tea. They wheeled her out here so she could get away from our mom. She and Mom are always having fights."

"Oh," said Calista. The woman wore an ancient dress that involved layer upon layer of black crepe and lace. She even wore black lace gloves and a hat with a spotted veil. She was Miss Havisham togged out in widow's weeds instead of bridal finery. "Does she always dress this way, or is it just for the funeral?"

"Always!" Maisie's immense blue eyes opened even wider.

"Ever since her husband died," Tigger said. "And that happened before we were born, before Mummy was born."

"Oh dear," said Calista.

"He shot himself," Tigger offered. "With a duck-hunting gun. Blew him right to pieces, Mummy said."

Calista looked down at the two beautiful little children. "My goodness." She was thinking how boring her stories must sound next to these of Mummy's. "Well, I bet she would appreciate cookies to wash down with her uh . . ."

"Brandy," Tigger offered. "Brandy and lemonade. That's what

she drinks. C'mon, Maisie," he said, tugging on his sister's hand. "This is boring."

Well, just get me in some black lace and give me a little brandy lemonade and a duck-hunting gun, Calista thought. But only briefly. She began making her way across the room.

"I am soooo glad you made your way to our side, my deah!" The little minnow eyebrows shot up with genuine delight. "I have been admiring your hair from afar."

"Oh, why thank you."

"And as Oscar Wilde once said, only a fool would not judge from appearances." He then giggled rather maniacally.

Calista was taken aback. Who was this dear soul with his quick wit and the most beautifully tied Windsor knot she had ever seen? She was utterly charmed. She extended her hand. "I'm Calista Jacobs."

"Calista Jacobs. Two lovely names. What could possibly connect you with anyone in this room?"

"Well, it's tenuous, but significant, I guess. I'm staying in the Baldwins' house."

"Oh my heavens." He slapped his pink cheek with a small white hand. "You're the one who discovered poor old Queenie"—his voice dropped—"shears and all!" He made a small grimace with his tiny mouth as if he was tasting something bad. "Well, I'm Rudy Kingsley, Queenie's brother-in-law, but before we go any further, let me introduce you to Titty."

Calista nearly choked on her Pimm's. "Who?"

"Titty, darling." He turned, bent over, and tapped on the shoulder of someone sitting in the armchair next to him who was engaged with another very elderly woman who looked more like a soggy tea bag than a living, breathing human being. Titty turned from the tea bag and looked up at Calista. It was a face that was simply unbelievable. Pudgy and wrinkled, she had bulging eyes that peered out from under very thick eyelids. With a flattened nose, the face appeared slightly reptilian. She was virtually neckless and her puffy jowls rested on a shirred collar reminiscent of Good Queen Bess. Unfortunately, Titty had decided to wear eye makeup. So a touch of lavender with flecks of gold floated across the thick lids. She looked like a gilded toad. "Ah!" she exclaimed in a voice that seemed squeezed out of her. "The lady of the hair."

"The lady of the hour, Titty."

"Queenie?" The small eyes behind the lavender lids swam with momentary confusion.

"Calista Jacobs, the one who discovered Queenie," Rudy whispered sotto voce.

"Oh my goodness!" The pudgy hand slapped a jowl. "How terrible for you, my deah. Oh heavens, and she's not even family. How awful for someone to have to become mixed up with us." She pulled out a hankie from somewhere and began to wipe beads of perspiration from her forehead. Whatever had she meant by that last remark? Calista wondered. "I hope you'll be all right. I mean, it must have been so shocking."

"Well yes, of course, but I'll be all right; that's hardly the issue. Unfortunately . . ."

"Yes, Queenie will not be all right. It's absolutely unfathomable. I just can't understand it."

"Look, look at Bootsie," Calista said suddenly. She spotted Bootsie. She was standing against the heavy velvet drapes and seemed almost to be receding into the deep folds. Her eyes, however, were feverish and they were looking directly at Bambi, who was standing close to Gus, across the room.

"That poor, poor girl." Rudy sighed.

"Oh Boots?" Titty said. "Yes, poor Boots. So fragile."

"Is she okay?" Calista asked. Bootsie's eyes were no longer locked on Gus and Bambi. Instead, they were darting about the room.

"She looks like she wants to get out, doesn't she?" Rudy said.

"Don't we all?" Titty replied.

"Let me go over and rescue her," Rudy said. "Bring her back over here to our little oasis of sanity. By the way, Calista, Cousin Titty and I believe ourselves to be the only sane ones of the whole crew." He leaned forward as if to huddle with Calista and Titty. "And that's not saying much—me being an old queen."

"And me a failed debutante!" Titty broke in.

Calista had the strangest feeling. In this stuffy old Victorian house, it was as if she had climbed up onto the mantel and looked into the mirror; and the glass, just as it had in Alice's story, became "all soft like gauze, melting away like a bright silvery mist" while she, Calista, had magically passed through it into another world, entered another dimension. Nothing seemed to be what it really was and these two very curious creatures—one, this . . . this Red Queen—were to be her guides! She watched Rudy as he scurried across the room toward Bootsie and gently led her over to Calista and Titty. Would the clocks start talking next? The pictures come alive, the cherubs jump from their frames, the bosomy court ladies spill from the oval panels and accost the gentlemen? Would the pharaohs at the Temple of Karnak climb from their tombs?

"Calista! Isn't that the most marvelous name. Well, as you know, I'm a sucker for anything Greek. We need to get everyone here a refill," Rudy announced, snapping his fingers to flag down a serving girl. "Pimm's here for Calista? What are you drinking, Boots—vodka?"

"No, no, just some white wine." That was interesting, Calista thought. From what she'd seen yesterday and what Gus had said, she would have guessed Bootsie to be into higher-proof stuff.

"Titty, I know you—sherry. Gawd, darling, how you do it in this heat, I'll never know. And just two fingers of scotch on the rocks with a twist for me." He nodded at the serving girl. Calista liked Rudy's way with the woman who brought the drinks. There was no condescension. It was strictly business, but there was a gentleness and respect for the young woman and the job, which couldn't have been an easy one. This was a man used to being around servants and running a household.

"Now you must tell us all about your name. As I was saying, I just love anything Greek—"

"And your hair . . ." Titty broke in.

"Oh come on, guys." Calista laughed. She couldn't believe it, but she was actually enjoying herself quite a bit, and she had dreaded coming.

"No, we're serious." Rudy rolled his eyes.

"Well, if I tell you that, you have to tell me about your tailor and your beautiful tie."

"Oh, I'm so glad you noticed." Rudy looked down at his magenta-and-blue tie with the tiny design. "Boots, darling, it's a Guards tie, belonged to an old intimate of mine. One only wears a Brigadier tie after six o'clock or at the annual wreath-laying in the Guards Chapel. I felt the occasion warranted it."

Calista was sure that Bootsie's eyes would spill celadon tears. She leaned forward and kissed Rudy on the cheek. "Thank you, Uncle Rudy," she whispered. Then she said, "You know, the least interesting thing about Calista is her name and her hair. She is a wonderful children's book artist."

"Oh my word . . . how marvelous."

Rudy and Titty were awash in convulsions of praise, although neither one had ever seen her work. "I knew you didn't fit in here; I just knew it!" Titty was saying. Apparently, in her mind, this was the highest compliment one could give.

"Tell me, dear, have you done any of the Greek myths for children?" Rudy was asking. Suddenly, it burst upon Calista who Rudy Kingsley was. All those statues, the lovely Greek torsos, the lovely Greek boys, indeed some of the major Hellenic pieces in the Museum of Fine Arts had been donated by R. W. Kingsley years ago. She had heard about him. She was sure Nan and Will Baldwin had mentioned him, now that she thought about it. She must call them tonight. They had already called, anxious about her safety and any news she might have about the murder.

"Oh my goodness!" Titty moaned. "She's coming our way."

"Who?" Calista asked.

"The meanest lady in Boston."

"I'm getting out of here," Bootsie said. "If she asks me about that fucking portrait one more time . . ."

"Oh gawd no! She's still on that?" Rudy sighed.

It was the lady in black lace being wheeled by her attendant toward them.

"Hello, darling Cornelia!" Rudy trilled.

"Don't you look ridiculous." The old lady growled and proffered a heavily powdered cheek for a kiss.

"Aren't you afraid I might have AIDS, darling?"

"What's that?"

"Ye gods!" Titty murmured.

It was at this juncture that Calista decided she should go. But neither Rudy nor Titty was letting her slip off without making a date. "Tomorrow noon, luncheon at the Ritz."

Why not? Calista thought, and accepted enthusiastically. It might be murder that had brought them together, but Rudy and Titty were about the most interesting people she had met in a long time.

"Titty? Her name is actually Titty?" Charley blinked in disbelief. They were back on Louisburg Square, eating Chinese takeout on the small terrace. Calista was grateful that an immense hedge of yew blocked the Kingsleys' greenhouse from her sight.

"You have to get used to it with these people. They all have funny nicknames—especially the women."

"Who was their dad, Walt Disney?"

"Well, I'll tell you one thing, Titty and Rudy are great. I think Gus is very nice, too, actually. So is Bootsie, for that matter. She just has a little drinking problem. What's her son like, by the way?"

"I don't know. He's a little weird. But he showed up to talk to them about working. He's got the job, as far as I can tell. They really do need people."

"How do you mean, weird?"

"I don't know just . . . you know, weird . . . like it's hard to explain just weird . . . you know . . ."

Calista had heard it all before, a kind of teenage aphasia, an inarticulate loop of monosyllabic jargon—*weird, cool, major weirdness, sucks.* These words were then punctuated at frequent intervals with *you know.* One became used to it as an elemental narrative form in what passed for conversation. Put these kids in a majorly cool nineteenth-century drawing room—like, you know, Jane Austen's and, you know . . . so much for literature. *Pride and Prejudice* down the toilet along with *Barchester Towers, Middlemarch,* and the rest of the majorly talky books of manners and morals.

They cleaned up after dinner. Charley helped administer the various medicines to Piss and Moan, then retired to his room, Archie's old room. Three nights a week, he was sys op, a systems operator on Channel 1, a computer bulletin board. He could sys-op out of wherever he happened to be as long as he set up the access. And he made twice as much money doing this as he did pedaling swan boats, but Calista had insisted that he do something in addition to computer work this summer. She lived in constant fear of raising an electronic nerd, and Charley had made great strides in the past few years, particularly since Archie had come into their lives.

Shortly after Tom had been killed, Charley had gone into a kind of withdrawal and seemed to derive all he needed from wandering the electronic mazes of computers. His best friends were electronic buddies on the other ends of modems. The world they shared was on bulletin boards, where they swapped information and played games. He was smart and he was skillful. From the time he was twelve, he had been programming freelance for departments around MIT and Harvard. When he was thirteen, he had worked in a summer program for talented Cambridge youth at the Martin Institute, a big cancer-research center. He had written a code with his friends Matthew and Louise for imaging crystallography in its application for protein folding in cellular structure. He had also become pale and soft. No more totally indoor summers, Calista vowed; hence, the swan boats.

Calista went into Will Baldwin's study, where she had set up her drawing board, and began to work on *The Emperor and the*

*Nightingale.* She had read many versions of the tale and then retold it in what she felt was a sparer way than some that seemed overly embellished. She was searching for a cadence both in words and illustration that came closest to haiku, or at least something that suggested East and not West in terms of storytelling. She had completed a dummy and now was beginning to work on the second big spread, the one that would have Quintana's needle juniper shrouded in fog. She took out the sketches she had made in the greenhouse on that last afternoon. She wanted the branches of the juniper to melt out of the mist. The negative space in this was more important than the positive. Somewhat like the enigma of Quintana, she suddenly thought. Indeed, the notion was so provocative that she put down her brush, which she was just preparing to dip in the ink wash.

What did she actually know of Quintana Parkington Kingsley? In so many ways, all of these Brahmins with their carefully constructed lives conducted in time-honored patterns carried out in venerable institutions and clubs seemed almost interchangeable. A tiny little world rotating in a tight orbit that moved in a peculiar rhythm related to nothing else. These lives were well documented in one sense because the orbits were so small and so predictable. There were no secrets, or were there? Calista picked up a page of her dummy, with a line of text running across the bottom. " *'Like bells of glass!' exclaimed the emperor. 'Like silver chimes! You must come and live and sing in my palace.'*

" *'But,' replied the nightingale, 'my song is far better among the green trees, the notes more beautiful in the fog of the morning, the rhythms dance with the stars of the open sky.' "*

Why did these lines suddenly have such resonance for Calista? Yes, it was a story of control, perfection, artifice, and finally genuine risk. It was about losing something. Why suddenly was she seeing those handless pictures of Bootsie's? The arms chopped off into stumpy nothingness swam in her mind.

There would be no drawing tonight. She needed to think. She went downstairs and poured herself a huge glass of ice water. The Chinese food had made her incredibly thirsty. She undressed and put on a light wrapper and went out onto the balcony with the ice water. It was a thick August night. The stars simmered in the sky. The moths seemed to sag in their swirling flights around the halos of outdoor garden lights. Calista thought about Bootsie, hopped-up eyes darting, darting as if she was trying to escape. She had seen that look before. Once years ago, she had gone to a reading by the poet Anne Sexton. Sexton was reading her poetry to the accompaniment of a jazz ensemble. The group was called Anne Sexton and Her Kind. It was an experience to hear her, to watch her. The throaty cigarette-thickened voice, the mad eyes sliding about the room as if to seek out the exits, the heat from her soul nearly palpable.

Calista got up suddenly. In the library downstairs, there was a shelf of poetry. Nan Baldwin was particularly fond of the confessional poets. She found them "refreshing." That, of course, was why Nan was not like half the woman Calista had seen at Diggory Parkington's on Marlborough Street that afternoon.

There was a row of Anne Sexton's books. Calista went right to *Transformations.* She owned the book herself. The poems were blistering reenactments of Grimm's fairy tales. As one of the foremost illustrators of fairy tales in the world, Calista was more than familiar with them. They were not all good poems by any means. They were indulgent often, superficial and a bit facile at times, but they were also unequivocally a dark plunge into the very belly of the fairy-tale beast. She opened the book right to the poem she wanted: "The Maiden Without Hands."

*Is it possible*
*he marries the cripple*
*out of admiration?*
*A desire to own the maiming. . . .*
*Lady, bring me your wooden leg*
*so I may stand on my own*
*two pink pig feet.*

The terrible words floated across the page with their immutable blood-drenched truth:

*Once*
*there was a cruel father*
*who cut off his daughter's hands*
*to escape from the wizard.*
*The maiden held her stumps*
*as helpless as dog's paws*
*and that made the wizard*
*want her. He wanted to lap*
*her up like strawberry preserve.*

Calista finished the poem and shut her eyes tightly. Something before murder had happened in this family. She was sure. Countless little murders, ones where there is no corpse—because the corpse is hidden, hidden in a facsimile of life. How clever.

And then out of the thick heat of the night, out of the soft charcoal darkness, another image floated toward Calista. She could barely perceive it. A boat with white flowers? No, with clouds, winged clouds? No, feathers. A swan boat. Would that make sense? No . . . no. She got up and found her sketch pad and flipped back through the pages. Here it was—the suggestion of a swan, in a tiny thumbnail sketch done with graphite and charcoal melting out of the smudged night—wings, a slender neck, created by the absence of darkness, by Calista rubbing with an eraser and sometimes with her own saliva.

"One could think of whores and not imagine the way of a swan . . ." Or was it "One could think of swans but not imagine the way of a whore . . ."? Did it come from Sexton? She thought so. She looked through *Transformations* but could not find the line. She went back to the shelf and searched in the other books. Still she could not find it. It had to be there someplace. She was sure. She would look again tomorrow. She was too tired now.

# 12

"People have sometimes called Oscar House a living museum. But I myself take offense at that," Rudy said primly, and patted his mouth with a beautiful paisley handkerchief after taking a sip from his martini. They were at a window table in the Ritz dining room, overlooking Arlington Street and the Public Garden. Rudy was well known at the Ritz. He had told Calista as soon as he sat down that although he always stayed at the Harvard Club, he ate most of his meals at the Ritz.

"Well, if you take offense, that's it!" Titty said in her small voice. "You dreamed the whole idea up. You can't imagine how lovely it is, Calista. On occasion, they make exceptions and allow women visitors."

"Oh, we certainly would for Calista. I can't think of a better candidate. You understand, I rather see Oscar House not as a living museum, and certainly not a memorial to Oscar Wilde—I mean I had to call it something—and although Wilde died in 1900 and I was not born until . . . well, some few years later, we did overlap in one small but significant way." Rudy's eyes glinted and fine lines creased the corners of his mouth as he smiled softly. Then his eyes seemed to grow dim, but the smile stayed. It was as if he were stepping back in time, through scores of years.

"One of Oscar's last lovers was my first. It was, shall we say, a seminal experience. Hence, Oscar House. I think of it as an academy, a place where young men—and now many have grown old—can come and think and play and study amongst beautiful things. But they were not just students. They were and are curators to all of these wonderful antiquities. It was required that they learn the art of conservation; the business of cataloging and assembling and displaying. Many of my 'graduates' have become curators and directors and appraisers around the world; speaking of which, I must try and contact Leon while I am here, even if I can't get down to New York."

"Leon? Leon Mauritz?" Calista asked.

"Yes, my dear. Do you know him?"

"I've met him just a couple of times. But Archie deals with him quite a bit."

"Of course, Archie Baldwin would—New World antiquities. And there's been so much looting. You can bet Leon will know who the buyers are." Rudy paused. "Yes, Leon is interesting in that sense."

Calista knew exactly what Rudy was talking about, for she had often heard Archie on the subject of Leon. For all intents and purposes, Mauritz operated scrupulously within the law, and particularly within the confines of the new ones prohibiting the selling of antiquities; he had, however, a profound knowledge of those who did not. As Archie had said more than once, with Leon there was only one side to be on—his good side.

"Well, I did not mean to digress here with Leon," Rudy resumed. "As I was explaining about Oscar House: Over the years as my collection grew, many of these pieces went out on loan to museums. You see, the residents of Oscar House lived amidst all this art and they were trained to care for it and were ultimately inspired by it."

"It's a theory, an aesthetic theory that Rudy has. He's written articles on it. The positive benefits from living in the midst of beauty, caring for it and all that."

"There's even a biofeedback doctor who has come to study the effects of it in terms of respiration and metabolism. I don't quite understand it, but apparently there is an ideal physiological set point for each body, and Dr. Watkins feels that the ideal proportions, et cetera, of Hellenistic art, in particular, can, in fact, induce healthful body rhythms.

"Even more than an academy, I think of Oscar House as a kind of library, along the lines of the great library of Alexandria. You know, a miniversion devoted to the antiquities and cultivating the kind of thought and aesthetic that can inspire creative minds. I founded it with my first real profits."

The waiter had just arrived and began to serve. Calista had cold salmon; Titty, the Ritz chicken salad; and Rudy, scrod. He looked down at his plate with the perfectly cooked piece of scrod, golden and plump in its thin crust of bread crumbs.

"This, of course, is a major reason for coming to Boston— scrod. The most unprepossessing of fish, called cod most other places, its numbers declining daily. But caught by our forebears for centuries and shipped salted-down in Kingsley vessels in the triangular trade. Ah, scrod!" Rudy's voice swelled with the encomium. "Well, cheers, ladies!" He lifted his martini in a jaunty salute.

"Rudy, what did you mean when you said your 'first real profits'?" Calista asked.

"Well, my dear, in our family, as in so many of these old Boston families, the fortunes were made in the last century. Substantial enough, they were nursed along and sometimes indeed did grow . . . but—"

"Rudy," interrupted Titty, "I can tell you're going to be much too modest about all this. To make a long story short, Rudy was the only person of his generation, possibly the last two generations, really to make money." Titty set down her fork. The gilded eyes sparkled and she raised her hands to emphasize her point.

The chubby fingers spread out in a fanlike gesture. "I mean really make money. How much was it, Rudy, with that drug firm in the Midwest?"

"Don't be coarse, Titty."

Titty dissolved in giggles over this. "You see, the whole point was that Rudy was supposed to be a fairy and fairies weren't supposed to have any head for money, and Kingie, Quintana's husband, was . . . you know—what's that word they use now for virile?"

"Macho," offered Calista.

"Yes. That's it, macho. And machos are supposed to make money. You know, do everything."

"Titty has a way of oversimplifying things," Rudy commented.

"Well, the point is that Kingie never made a dime of his own and our own little fairy here"—she turned and patted Rudy on the shoulder—"has made all the dough!"

"Did you do it all through the stock market?" Calista asked.

"Oh heavens, no. A lot through the art world. I began collecting stuff just for that purpose—you know, things that I knew I would never want as part of the family."

"That's what he calls his antiquities—the family."

"Like what?"

"Oh, for example, I never really liked de Kooning—but I knew his stuff would catch on. Same with Rothko. Then I made an awful lot in real estate."

"You see, they hate to admit that someone with—as they always said—Rudy's tendencies could make money and be a good businessman."

"Business fairy," Rudy said, and they both were seized by raucous fits of giggles. Rudy then took out the beautiful handkerchief from his breast pocket and wiped the tears from his eyes. "Oh my dear, you have no idea what it was like, what it is still like in one of these old families."

"No . . . no," said Calista softly, and she thought of the handless maiden and "a desire to own the maiming."

"Are you all right?" Both Rudy and Titty leaned forward at

once, alarmed by the sudden change in Calista's face. Calista bit her lip lightly. "What happened to Bootsie?" There was almost a stricken look in Titty's face, and Rudy reached out and patted her plump hand that lay as limp as a dead fish on the peach tablecloth. "And Muffy, Bootsie's sister? She died of alcoholism?"

Rudy squared his shoulders and looked straight ahead. "She died because she put a rope around her neck and hung herself." Titty squeezed her eyes shut as if to banish a terrible picture.

"I'm . . . I'm . . ." Calista stammered. "I'm so sorry I brought this up."

"There is no need to be sorry," Rudy said dryly. Titty gave him a furtive look. Rudy now sighed deeply. "There is a long history of troubled women in our family, and one cannot help but wonder if in some way Quintana's death is a continuation of that trouble."

"Troubles!" Titty seemed to come back to life. "You're sounding positively Irish, Rudy. You know, one always thinks of the Irish as so emotional, but when it comes to the really major things, Northern Ireland, for example, they refer to it as 'the troubles.' Or I remember a lovely Irish lady, a seamstress I used to go to. She referred to Hitler as 'the problem.' She had a sister in County Clare—you know, back then nobody knew how far Hitler might go. 'The problem'! she called him!" Titty's voice rose with indignation.

"I'm sorry, Titty dear. I didn't mean to belittle."

"Oh, Rudy, of course not. I know you better than that." She now reached over and patted his hand.

"Well, do you think that all this somehow relates to Quintana's murder?" Calista asked.

"Oh, it's hard to imagine." Rudy shook his head.

"Do the police have any ideas?" Titty asked. "I mean, obviously robbery was not a motive and there is no sign that the person broke in."

"Well, that is a moot point in a sense," Rudy offered, "seeing as she was working in the greenhouse, to which there are numerous access ways through the Connecting Gardens, no doubt."

"Exactly," said Calista. "If you could get into the gardens, it would be no trouble getting into the greenhouse. There are two doors—one directly out into the gardens and the other connecting to the house itself."

"So we can not assume that she must have known who it was and simply let the person in. A stranger could have gotten into the greenhouse easily enough and found her there," Rudy said.

"But why would a stranger come and murder her there if he didn't want to steal something?" Titty said. "Oh Lord, if she had only gone up to Nohqwha. She could have stayed at Bambi's on the other side of the island until the construction was over."

"I don't think Quintana cared for Bambi any more than the rest of us."

"What's with Bambi?" Calista asked.

"Oh nothing really—I guess. Except she's rather like her grandmother Cornelia. And people can never forgive women like Cornelia."

"Why?" Calista asked.

"Because she survived unscathed," Titty said simply.

Survived what? The question was left begging. But Calista didn't quite have the nerve to ask it. Rudy and Titty together presented a strange mixture of resignation, bitterness, and nerves that discouraged Calista from prying. These vague references to histories of troubles were not to be dismissed with a pat diagnosis of alcoholism. They were holding something back. She was sure. But now was not the time to push.

Calista returned to 16 Louisburg Square. She worked for the rest of the afternoon. Charley came home and reported that Jamie had indeed shown up for work and been hired. Charley had plans to go to a concert on the Esplanade with Matthew. Matthew would come back and spend the night with Charley. Calista was glad. The more people in the house, the better she felt.

Then why had it taken her forever to fall asleep? And when she did it had seemed like only a minute before she heard the goddamn cats. She got up and staggered downstairs, silently cursing the felines. They were both standing in an ivy bed screeching at a sliver of a moon. "C'mon, c'mon, guys. Calm down." She carried a saucer of milk laced with sherry. "Piss, come here. You lead the way. C'mon, boy."

Oh God, Calista thought. She really didn't understand cats at all. She picked up Moan and began to carry her toward the back door. She hoped Piss would follow. Then suddenly, it hit Calista. The last time, the only other time the cats had freaked like this in the middle of the night in the garden was the night of Quintana's murder. Had something, in fact, set them off—someone coming into the Connecting Gardens, over the walls, or perhaps from another house? The thought struck her forcibly. Anybody could have access to the gardens, just like herself, from another house. They wouldn't even have to go over the walls—just walk out a back door. She stood frozen to the ground. She looked around. The houses looked summer-vacant. The automatic lights turned on every evening. Calista subconsciously even knew the patterns of how the owners varied the sequence of when the clock timers would go off in the various rooms—to confuse would-be thieves, to suggest occupancy.

She clutched the cat tighter and began to walk toward the Kingsley greenhouse. The door was slightly ajar, not necessarily as if someone had just walked through but, rather, as if it had not closed properly. No wonder. There was one hinge separated from the door frame. It didn't look as if it had been forced. The hinge was old and rusty, one screw missing, the other screw half out of the hole. Moan was now calmed down and purring ever so softly in her arms. Piss stood on the low stone wall and looked disapprovingly at them. But Calista felt strangely emboldened. She wanted to see the greenhouse again. She looked over her shoulder at Piss and thought, Fuck you, then stepped through the door. She could get through sideways without even moving it.

Inside, it had all been swept up and washed down. Not a trace of the shattered needle juniper, nor a drop of Quintana's blood left. The Crime Scene people had obviously gotten all they needed. So why was she here? What more was there to find? Or was there something to look at again? She knew what it was. She wanted to see those pictures, the handless drawings of Bootsie's and Muffy's. They held a key, not to the murder but to the family.

She had given up thinking that these families were simple. How could she have ever thought that? Look at Archie's family. There were enough nuts in the Baldwins—certain branches of the family, that was—to start a small posh mental clinic. So, she told herself, she was not really trying to solve a murder but, rather, do a little ethnographic research and maybe just help somebody, somebody like Bootsie, who seemed so terribly vulnerable. In these pursuits, was she not following some age-old practices of previous generations of Bostonians? Was there not a touch of the settlement-house ethic here—repairing damaged souls? Why was she so sure that Bootsie had been damaged?

Calista had been walking slowly through the rows of dwarfed plants toward the connecting door to the main house when suddenly she heard footsteps. She froze and gripped Moan to her chest. The steps became louder. She heard a door from the pantry open. There wasn't time to get out of the greenhouse. Where would she hide? There was hardly camouflage among these stupid dwarf plants. In a corner, she spotted some fifty-pound bags of peat moss and fertilizer for spreading in the Connecting Gardens, no doubt. She rushed over. There was just enough room to wedge herself and Moan behind them. She crouched and tried to steady her breathing. Her heart was pounding ferociously and Moan, unlike herself, evidently found it soothing, for the dear old cat had nestled close to Calista's breast and for all intents and purposes seemed to have fallen asleep. Whoever it was had now entered the greenhouse. Calista could hear the click of heels on the brick. The knowledge dawned slowly. Those clicks must be from a woman's shoes—high heels. Just at that moment, they stopped within a yard of where Calista crouched. She could see the legs. Long and well shaped, they were sheathed in stockings with seams! Who wore stockings with seams anymore? Maybe prostitutes with garter belts. Calista's eyes opened in disbelief.

She indeed spotted the buckle at the end of a strap. The woman was crouching down near the spot where Quintana's body had lain. She was running a gloved hand over the bricks as if searching for something. With her skirt hiked up, the buckle at the end of the strap showed and then popped. "Shit!" the voice muttered. Then with her right hand holding up the top of the stocking, she hitched the garter buckle to the fabric. There was something very sexy about the entire move. Maybe that's why men went crazy for straps and garters and all that outmoded paraphernalia. The woman then got up, continued out the back greenhouse door, and into the Connecting Gardens. Piss went nuts and began screeching again. But the figure hurried on. Calista rose up a bit and had a clear view. The woman was dressed in a somewhat old-fashioned-style dress or suit that showed off an hourglass figure. Her shoulders looked fairly broad, but her waist was very narrow and so were her hips. The hair appeared light in color and brushed her shoulders. She carried a tote, which jiggled against her hip as she tottered across the Connecting Gardens. Maybe it was the uneven bricks or perhaps her heels were too high, but she reminded Calista of herself when she had first worn high heels as a youngster and was not used to the new balance required for walking. She then disappeared around a hedge. Presumably, she went out through one of the tunneled alleyways that opened onto Pinckney Street. Only residents had keys to the doors at either end. Calista herself had Heckie's, the Baldwins' manservant.

Calista came out from behind the peat and fertilizer bags. She felt stiff and almost cold, although her body was sweaty from sheer nerves. The temperature must have dropped. When the cooler air hit her perspiring skin, it sent a chill through her. She was standing near the place where the woman had crouched. What had she been looking for? She began to walk toward the door, still clutching the sleeping Moan, when she spotted the silvery thing wedged between two bricks. She bent down and picked it out. It was a garter buckle, separated from the strap. Calista held it lightly and tried to figure out what the significance was. All she could think was that somewhere in Boston there was a lady with a great figure running around with one stocking about to fall down. No wonder she had said "Shit" when the other garter popped. Was this evidence? Evidence of what? Evidence perhaps that she, Calista, had illegally entered the Kingsley house and had seen a stylish woman there at 2:30 in the morning. This was going to be a hard one to explain to the police.

# 13

"Do we really have to eat lunch with him?" Matthew was asking Charley as they headed toward the swan boats. It would be two hours before the boats opened for the public, but it took nearly all that time to get them wiped down, organize the ticket rolls, and go over the scheduling changes.

"Well, hopefully Art will put him on a different shift so our lunch breaks won't be the same," Charley said.

"I mean, it's not that he's not nice. But he's just so weird. He's kind of a heavy presence to have around." Matthew paused. "Especially in this heat. Why aren't we working in an air-conditioned office?"

"Because our mothers were afraid we were becoming nerdy, and apparently fresh air is an inhibitor of nerdiness. I'm sorry I got you involved with this Jamie guy, but I guess I sort of felt sorry for him. He does strike you as kind of a terminal loser."

"There's just something kind of dark about him. I don't mean dark in a bad way, like evil, just, you know—heavy, depressing. Like I mean, I know his grandmother got murdered and everything, but I still think he's just plain weird."

"No doubt about it, but you should see the rest of his family. They're all weird. His mom's an alcoholic—at least that's what my mom told me. And did I tell you about this lady who my mom says is really charming and she likes a whole bunch?"

"No. Who's that?"

"Get this: Her name is Titty—Aunt Titty."

"Titty!" Matthew gasped. "As in boobies, breasts, knockers?" He stopped dead in his tracks on the sidewalk that led from the Charles Street gate to the pond. They were right in front of the statue of Edward Everett Hale. "I need support," Matthew said, leaning on the pedestal. He began to laugh hysterically. "Titty! Titty!" He was screaming. "They named her Titty. How could parents do that to a kid?" He was doubled over and tears were running down his cheeks. A businessman walking by briskly with a briefcase glanced their way.

"It's funny, Matthew, but not really that funny." But then Charley began to laugh, too. They had both collapsed just under Mr. Hale's feet and walking stick.

"I don't think we should ever complain again about something our parents might do," Matthew said, gasping. "I mean, look— we've got these nice solid plain names, and who cares if we have to pedal two tons of fiberglass swan around in ninety-eight degrees of heat—piece of cake next to TITTY!"

"Nothing to live up to," Charley said, and started laughing again.

"Or out to," Matthew said, cupping his hands in front of his chest to indicate enormous breasts.

"Oh gross."

They finally picked themselves up. "Well, at least Jamie doesn't have a weird name. So what's his excuse?" Matthew asked.

"Well, his parents are divorced, and as I was saying, his mom's alcoholic and his grandmother just got murdered. So that's a nice little starter kit toward weirdness. But I get the feeling he was this way before."

"He's so silent and he's always biting his nails—you notice that?"

"Yeah, and sometimes it's almost like he doesn't hear you. I swear it's like his mind is totally elsewhere. He gets this totally far-off look in his eyes."

"Why did you ever tell him about this job?"

"Well, I don't know. I mean, we *are* short of help. It means we don't have to do double trips and can actually take full-size lunch breaks, and you know, I was just standing there with him and, as you notice, this guy isn't really talky. I was sort of grasping at straws for conversation and it just came up."

"You know, Jacobs, you really might have a career as a social worker."

"Forget it. I don't want to have to spend my days talking to weird people."

"Well, maybe you should join the clergy. I mean, you have this do-good streak. Become a rabbi."

"I don't think rabbis or any other ministers have a do-good streak. Besides, I'm an agnostic."

"How can you be an agnostic? You're Jewish."

Charley stopped again. "Hold it right there. You can too. My grandfather said so. I am a Jewish agnostic."

"Impossible."

"Not at all: You eat Jewish; you think Jewish; you basically follow the Ten Commandments. And if you believed in God, you would only believe in one."

"Sounds kind of half-baked to me."

"All agnostics are half-baked. My dad was an agnostic—sort of."

"What do you mean 'sort of'?"

"He basically believed that God was a simplification of a lot of laws that underlie particle physics—a lot of laws and stuff we haven't discovered yet. I think my dad really did believe in God. I think he thought God was at the bottom of Cygnus II and a lot of other black holes he spent his life studying. I know he thought there was a God particle in there somewhere."

"A God particle," Matthew mused.

"Yeah, that's what we agnostics think. It's not that we don't believe in God. It's just that we don't believe the God particle can be explained—at least not in a church or synagogue, or not for a moral benefit."

Charley, Matthew thought, was truly amazing sometimes. He didn't know where he got these ideas. But they popped up all the time.

Charley had just finished unloading his fifth boatload of "swannies." He saw Matthew, who had been working the ticket line, standing off to one side with Jamie. There was a tall, slender man standing with them as he walked up.

"Oh, hello. Charley Jacobs, right?" He leaned forward and extended his hand. "Gus Kingsley, Jamie's uncle. I was just in this neck of the woods and I thought I might stop by and take Jamie for lunch. But he says he already has plans."

"I think that's an excellent idea," a woman said, coming up suddenly. "Why don't you let Jamie be with his new friends? You really don't belong here," she said quite pointedly.

"Mom, what are you doing here?" Jamie's dark eyes never looked up from the asphalt path. Then, under his breath and barely audible, he added, "What is everyone doing here?"

"Uh . . . well . . ." Matthew was saying. "We didn't mean to—"

"Nonsense," Bootsie broke in. "You fellows have your plans. There is no place around here for us."

"Then what are you all doing here?" Jamie spat out the words, turned, and, hunching his shoulders, walked off in the opposite direction.

Bootsie looked off, following him with her eyes. She raised her hand and lightly touched her cheek. It was a gesture of confusion mixed with utter despair. Gus, aware of the two boys standing there rather dumbfounded, tried to recoup from the awkwardness of the moment. "Well, I guess we adults have a knack for just marching in sometimes at the wrong moments." He reached out to shake both Matthew's and Charley's hands and gave them each a very earnest gaze. "I'm sorry, boys, really sorry." He looked again almost questioningly into Charley's eyes, and Charley could not help but wonder what he was looking for. It seemed to be more than understanding. Bootsie, meanwhile, was busy lighting up a cigarette, her eyes darting about like a freaked starling in a sudden gust. A genuine loony-tune, thought Charley.

# 14

It was Friday morning and the weekend loomed ahead like a great two-day yawn. Charley and Matthew had the entire weekend off, their first all summer. Matthew had invited Charley down to the Cape, where his parents had a home. Calista was chained to her drawing board. Her plans were to really push for the next four days and then take a long weekend in Vermont beginning the following Thursday. But at the moment, she was feeling terrifically sorry for herself. Everyone else was someplace summery and having fun. Her own parents had called up to urge her to fly out to Montana, where they rented a cabin every summer for two weeks of fly-fishing on the Madison River. Nan and Will Baldwin called every few days with tempting invitations to come up to Mount Desert Island. But Calista was behind, and Janet Weiss, her editor, was nervous.

Nothing was cooperating, however. In the humid thickness of the August morning, the India ink full of shellac was hardening up faster than usual. It seemed as if every fifteen minutes her pen was getting clogged and she was having to take a razor blade to it.

Then to add to that, she was working on vintage Whatman paper, the kind people killed for. Calista had not had to kill for it. Her dear old friend and mentor Emma Plotkin, a consummate children's book artist, had died at the age of eighty-six the previous winter and had actually willed to Calista and another young artist a stash of Whatman board bought in the year 1952. It was the paper that had inspired Calista to do this retelling of *The Emperor and the Nightingale.* Old Whatman, a cold-press-plate paper, was rather like red wine; it got better with age. It had a soft buttery yellow cast. It absorbed the ink perfectly for the feel that Calista was striving for in this story. It seemed to be paper looking for the right story. And Calista knew the Chinese fairy tale of Hans Christian Andersen, full of nuance and quiet passion, was the story. But it had also been problematic.

She was not just serving the story to the paper, however; this was a tribute to Emma. She felt Emma's spirit hovering around her always when she came to work on the book. And although that spirit was a benign one, it was nonetheless inhibiting. For one thing, she had a very limited supply of this paper—just enough for three books. So she couldn't screw things up. This was why it had taken her so long to get going. Every morning, there was half an hour of agony before her drawings seemed to loosen up, her hands relax. She didn't even work on the paper for the first forty-five minutes. She did a series of sketches and scribbled on other stuff she had around. But now the goddamn shellac was getting hard as nails in the ink. The fisherman pulling in his nets under the moon in his boat on the lake where the nightingale sang did not look right, not at all. Just then, the phone rang. Calista picked it up.

"Rudy here, dear. How are you doing?"

"Ecch!" Calista made a sound halfway between a snort and a whine.

"Not good. I can tell. How about a jaunt to the country with Titty and me? We have to go up to Nohqwha to check on the work Queenie was having done. It's apparently finished, and Gus can't make it and Bootsie isn't in any shape to. It's so nice when octogenarians can be helpful. I've got a car and a driver."

"Well, I could certainly drive you. No need for you to spend that sort of money," Calista found herself saying while staring at the fisherman with his nets. Jesus, the moon didn't even look right in this drawing. She better quit while she was ahead. "How long are you going for?"

"Oh, we'll come back tomorrow, late afternoon."

"All right," she said.

At least it wouldn't be the whole weekend. It might be fun and maybe it would give her a chance to talk to Titty some more. She had never exactly figured it out after reading that Sexton poem about the handless maiden. She thought again of those drawings. There was indeed a sense of mutilation in this family, of perhaps countless little murders, or corpses—so well hidden because they came sheathed in the accoutrements of life. And then she thought of the nightingale she would soon be drawing—the real living, breathing one that the emperor wanted to possess completely and the bejeweled artificial one with its glittering plumage studded with diamonds and rubies and its mechanical song locked in its breast, to be released only when the emperor wound the key. Both the poem about the handless maiden and *The Emperor and the Nightingale* were stories of control, or the lust for perfect and complete control.

She had found the Sexton poem with the swans and the whore. It was called "Song for a Red Nightgown." She had read it and thought of Bootsie. But she still did not know why. She could not understand what the poem meant. But when she came to the lines "One could think of feathers and/not know it all. One could/ think of whores and not imagine the way of the swan," Calista thought of Bootsie. She knew that there was a link between this poem and Bootsie and possibly the death of Quintana Kingsley. She felt that Titty knew part of the answers she sought. There was so much to sort out: swans and nightingales, red nightgowns and whores, Brahmins and bonsai. And survivors—what was it that Titty had said about Cornelia and Bambi being survivors? Where did the survivors fit in with all this?

There was no doubt about it: Rudy knew how to do things in style. He would not hear of her driving. He had rented a Bentley, and one of the stewards from the Harvard Club who had the weekend off had been hired to drive. Commodious and well upholstered, it was much more suited for the two octogenarians than Calista's Subaru or her old VW Bug that she hung on to simply because she could not bear to part with it. Archie had felt it terribly dangerous and bought her the Subaru as a Hanukkah present—at least that was what he'd said it was for. Titty, who was of ample proportions, would have found the Subaru a squeeze, however. So the three of them were now riding north in splendor on Route 93 toward New Hampshire. Rudy was sitting in the front seat with the driver and had an array of maps spread out before him. He also carried a compass. He and Titty were having a spirited discussion on how they used to get to Nohqwha seventy years earlier.

"No, we'd take the steamer from India Wharf, and in the morning we'd wake up at the Isles of Shoals and then Talbot would pick us up in the coach."

"Titty, you're all wrong. When Talbot worked for my father, they already had the Studebaker."

"Studebaker—that's a very modern automobile, Rudy. I think it might have been a Packard."

"Well, it wasn't a coach, I'll tell you that. I think maybe when we were infants, my parents had a manservant named Apollo who used to drive their coach. And then he became their chauffeur. That's what a lot of these old coachmen did."

"Well, in any case, that last part always seemed to take forever. I just remember jumping up and down in what I picture as a coach, asking when we were going to get there."

"Now will you explain to me once again how you and Rudy are cousins?" Calista asked.

dress up like women?" He paused and plucked a blade
"It would seem that this phenomenon is a peculiar con-
n of urges, insecurities, and . . . and, yes, I do believe in
es, mean-spiritedness."
 was watching Titty, who was rapt with attention.
dressing up," Rudy continued, "the way they do it, is
y a mockery, yet it's something they need to do. I have
ose up. I worked the lights backstage at the Welles;
ild get out there myself. But I saw those men. They
 more masculine than when they were flexing their
n tutus and stuffing their jockstrapped cocks into
They were mocking, putting down the other sex. But at
ime, they were saying, 'There but for the grace of God
 yet . . ." He paused again. "And yet, some craved it.
have they done in those shows? They have created a
*ant* not of femininity but of humiliation. They want to
umiliation—it is, after all, a direct escape from the
their caste, the exigencies of their pedigree."
!" Titty exploded.
heir whole notion of masculinity is sick, if you ask
huffed, made a moue with his lips, and shrugged. "I
 to our dear relative."
 It was a statement, not a question.
eedy, Titty. The Reverend himself."
lista suddenly recalled, "Queenie had a portrait of
Mather."
d Titty, "and it is the one Cornelia is lusting after.
 the family are directly related to the old creep."
double dose, as it 'twere," Rudy said, and stretched
"I always loved what Marion Starkey, the historian
bout the Salem witch trials, said about Cotton

that?" asked Calista.
, Miss Starkey suggested that if the witchcraft ex-
't happened, Cotton Mather would have had to in-
his zeal for discovering witches. It was not some-

"My mother's sister Abigail married Tad Kingsley, Kingie's
and Rudy's father. Abigail and Tad were much better off than my
parents, of course. But Abigail convinced Tad to lease us some
land at a very low cost. My father, Horace, was an architect and
built a lovely camp on it."

"Is it still there?" Calista asked.

"No, no. It burned—when was that, Rudy?"

"Oh, before the war, I think."

"Wait—when was Pearl Harbor?"

"Oh, it was long before that, Titty."

On and on they went, trying to reconstruct an evanescent past,
with details that had seemed to wash away like watercolors, having left unreadable but nonetheless indelible stains.

They stopped for lunch near Lake Ossipee, at a spot Rudy remembered. Malcolm, their chauffeur, got out the hamper from
the trunk. Calista was helping Titty out of the car.

"There's no picnic table, Titty. Will you be okay on the
ground?"

"Oh, we brought Titty's portable chaise," Rudy said from the
rear of the car. "Malcolm will be right there with it."

"Isn't he a dear?" Titty sighed. "And have you ever seen anything more adorable?" She gazed with rapture at her cousin, who
was standing by the trunk with his walking stick as he supervised
the unloading for the picnic.

Calista had to admit she hadn't. Rudy was an elfin picture of
sartorial perfection in his pale tan poplin knickerbockers, pink-
striped shirt and red suspenders, an ascot of tiny checks tucked
in the neck of the shirt, and, to top it all off, a bright white cap
with a small brim.

Malcolm brought the folding chaise over for Titty and he and
Rudy set it up. Titty eased her great bulk into it.

"Comfy, my dear?" Rudy asked.

"Of course—fit for a queen."

"Yes." Then Rudy turned to Calista. "I was once at Cowes
Week with Lord Abington—very close to the Queen Mum, he is,
and she was there, too. We took tea with her on the royal yacht,

and instead of a deck chair, she had one of these. I immediately called up Hawes and Groot. They are actually sailmakers but have done very well in safari gear and that sort of thing; they can do anything with canvas or Dacron, and they'd done the Queen Mother's chair. So I ordered one for Titty."

"You always take care of me, dear." She reached for Rudy's hand and pressed it to her plump cheek. It was the tenderest gesture.

"And I always will." Rudy looked down on his cousin with a look of pure love. He then reached into the cooler. "I'll be the wine steward. It's so much fun doing it outside," Rudy said. "Malcolm, you get the rest ready. We're going to serve the vichyssoise in those big goblets. No spoons required. You can just drink up, kiddos, and let's see, we have loads of smoked salmon sandwiches—some with the dill sauce, some without. And there's potato salad." Rudy stopped and slapped his cheek. "Oh Gawd, that's rather redundant, isn't it? Vichyssoise and potato salad! How'd I ever do that? You know, aside from losing one's looks, getting old is really a pain in the old arse when one makes slips like these. I know this isn't the worst—here, try this, darling." He had just uncorked a bottle of wine and was pouring some into a glass for Calista. "It's a Montrachet. Anyway, as I was saying—" He stopped abruptly. "Oh, I shouldn't complain. I've really had a wonderful life against all odds."

"Against all odds?" Calista asked.

"Oh yes, my dear. It really is against all odds when you're born into a family like this."

"Absolutely." Titty nodded and held out her glass to Rudy. He poured the wine.

"You're born into what is commonly thought of as great privilege. It's really, however, something to overcome. You must make your own luck and tiptoe through the privilege. So it is against all odds and despite all privilege."

"Oh, I like that, Rudy!" Titty exclaimed, and raised her glass. "Here's to figuring out the odds and tiptoeing through the privilege."

At this point, Rudy began ti wineglass aloft, and singing an "Tiptoe Through the Tulips." T with bloodlines, Cabots, Welds and opium fortunes, Beacon H laughing gleefully and Calista she was in and how much nice India wash from clogging her p

"You see!" cried Titty, aln Welles Club missed somethin;

"If I'm going to dress up li one of those god-awful tarty venchy." Rudy ran one han svelte waist. "Audrey Hepbu

"What's this about the We Welles Club, along with the one of the handful of clubs t all else was to fall into its These archaic old clubs we cial structure. Unlike New eschewed the plush masc were distinctly austere in merchant princes and sc overt simplicity, they pos the scheme of things. An the Tavern, let down its I

"They call it the 'Friv dress up as chorines an( the Hasty Pudding Clul

"Oh how stupid," C; folderol used to drive ( serious physics studen

"More than stupid, him and was sipping h

"How do you mean'

"It is an interestin

clubmer
of grass.
catenati(
some cas
Calist;
"This
essentiall
seen it c
never wo
never fel
muscles
bloomers.
the same t
go I.' And
And what
tableau viu
toy with h
burdens of
"It's sicl
"Very—
me." Rudy
trace it bac]
"Cotton."
"Yes, ind
"Oh," Ca
him, Cotton
"Yes," sa
Both sides o
"We got a
out his legs.
who wrote a
Mather."
"What was
"As I reca]
perience had]
vent it, given

thing he would have foregone, she said; for it was, in fact, 'the scarlet thread drawn through the drab New England homespun.' Rather like the kick those fellows get with their corsets."

"Yes," said Titty. "And of course, women are always the victims."

"Always," Rudy said quietly.

# 15

The houses and summer bungalows became sparser and the woods thicker. The road grew narrower and soon the tar turned to dirt. Ahead, Calista could glimpse a patch of sparkling water. "There it is—Lake Sachem!" Rudy exclaimed.

"I hope Hoops is there with the boat," Titty said.

"Oh, he will be. Has Hoops ever failed?"

"True," said Titty.

"We need a boat to get there?" Calista asked.

"Oh yes," Rudy said. "You see Nohqwha is on an island in the middle of Lake Sachem."

"It must be a big lake," Calista said.

"Oh it is. And the island is big, too. Do you know why it is called Nohqwha?" Rudy turned around in the front seat to talk to Calista.

"No idea. Why?"

"It's an old Seneca tale, one of those stories about the small one, the runt of the litter, winding up the all-powerful one. In this story, the little boy runs off to where he shouldn't go, a dangerous land, and he hears what he thinks are people calling, 'My Father! My Father!' And he fears that they are going to kill his father. But in truth, it was not people at all. It was frogs singing the frog song—'*Nohqwha! Nohqwha!*' This story caught my grandfather's fancy and—you know, this was back in the days of romance about the Indians—many of the great Adirondack camps had Indian names. So Grandfather named our place Nohqwha. There are lots of frogs around—frog tapestries, weavings, little frog statues, door knockers. You know how a lot of people get about their summer places—little themes, leitmotifs, secret handshakes—all very Cub Scouty, really. So our totem, so to speak, is the frog."

Calista wasn't sure. Her vacation home in Vermont did not have a name. She never had thought of naming it. It didn't have a theme, either. "Well," she said, "I was always crazy about Jeremy Fisher. For years, I've been trying to buy one of Beatrix Potter's studies of Jeremy. No luck."

"You don't say?" Rudy turned around and lifted a minnow eyebrow. "You deal with Ropes and Fremont, Kensington High Street, for that sort of thing?"

"Yes. How'd you know?"

"Oh, the things I know are surprising, my dear," he said cryptically. "Ah! Here we are, and there is our good fellow Hoops."

They had arrived at a pier that stretched out into glassy dark water. When Calista stepped outside the car, it was slightly chilly. It was wonderful. She could feel the heat, the fumes, the grit of the city peel off of her like layers of old skin. The scent of spruce was in the air.

"It feels wonderful!" Titty sighed and stood resting her weight on her tripod cane. A slight breeze now riffled the water. At the end of the pier, Calista spotted a shell—double-ended, slightly wide for a true racing shell, but with more flowing lines than a rowboat. It was precisely what she had been attempting to draw that morning, just hours before. It even had a little birch canopy. This was a sign, she decided, that it had indeed been wise for her to leave her drawing board and come to New Hampshire, to Lake Sachem, and glide in a boat across the mirrored water to Nohqwha.

Calista was big on signs that permitted her to do what she really wanted to do. The first time she ever slept with Archie, it was a sign that she needed to move on to something else when she had been stuck on a drawing for *Marian's Tale,* a revisionist telling of Robin Hood. It had actually been a drawing of Marian shooting a bow and arrow that had her stumped. When Archie had arrived on that hot summer night, Charley was away and she was wearing running shorts, with no underpants underneath. What could have been clearer? This lady needed to get laid by someone who cared about her and whom she cared about deeply. So she just invited him into her study, and the next thing she knew, they were on the floor and Marian was still on the drawing boards, looking envious. She finished the picture the next day. It was lovely on all counts.

Hoops, although decrepit in appearance, had a sprightly gait and quickly loaded their bags into the boat. Titty's chaise was unfolded. It fit perfectly into the middle section of the boat. She looked like a benevolent toad queen surveying her domain. Rudy reclined in a slant-back low seat in the bow, looking positively louche. Calista decided he was one of those people who despite rather bizarre first impressions and general appearance can actually fit in anywhere and look as if he belonged. Calista sat on a seat in the stern under the birch-bark canopy and felt as if she were a character in one of her own fairy tales.

Once upon a time, thought Calista, this had been a tent, or perhaps two or three on platforms with canvas flaps. But now what loomed before Calista as they walked from the pier up the pine path was a rustic creation that blended elements of a Swiss chalet with an American frontier log cabin. A fanned gable thrust out over a deep front porch. The rail of the porch was a spectacular intaglio of bent, peeled birch limbs. On the second level was another balcony with equally intricate railwork. Living trees had been incorporated directly into the porch structure of the house, with two great hemlocks on either end forming posts. The simplicity of the rustic log-cabin design combined with an ornamentation that was clearly Swiss was pure Adirondacks style and indeed perfect for this woodland-lake setting.

"Oh, they did a marvelous job on the upper verandas, Hoops."

"Well, sir, they spent a heck of a long time steaming that wood to make it bend. They knew what they were doing."

"Real craftsmen."

"Too bad Mrs. Kingsley couldn't see it. She was a passel of nerves about those verandas. Think it was where Mr. Kingsley used to romance her."

"Yes, yes," said Rudy somewhat hastily. Calista caught a glimpse of Titty and her breath locked in her throat. The eyes behind the thick lids were glittering, hard little slits, like narrow windows that showed a hatred that was so intense, it seemed to sear the very air around them.

Calista's bedroom was a Spartan affair just to her liking: a narrow pine bed, a chest of drawers with a small partially deglazed mirror above it, a braided rug on the floor, a small desk, a dear little twig nightstand supported by curved birch branches. On top was a reading light and a book of Rupert Brooke poetry on a crocheted doily. How odd! Calista thought, picking up the book. Who ever read Rupert Brooke nowadays? But as she opened the book and a pressed corsage fell out, she knew. This had to have been Muffy's book. It was as if time had stopped here and she had an uncanny sense that this was Muffy's room. This must have been Muffy's room. She looked around with renewed interest.

She heard a gong clang two times.

"Oh my stars and garters!" squeaked Titty, who stood outside the open door to Calista's room.

"What's that?" Calista asked.

"Rudy—Uncle Rudy, camp director of Nohqwha. He loves doing this. Two gongs mean time for a swim."

"It's kind of chilly, isn't it?"

"Of course it is. But why should that stop you? We're in the woods, lovey, plenty of plain living and high thinking. It will clear the brain, and if you don't do this, they might give you a physic or, worse yet, an enema." The eyes narrowed again to the little slits with the hard light. But then she laughed merrily.

"Are you going swimming?" Calista asked.

"In a manner of speaking," Titty replied.

Titty's manner of swimming was to recline in an Avon inflatable life raft and be rowed around in front of the swimming beach by Hoops, while trailing a languid hand in the water. Meanwhile, Rudy paddled about in a bathing suit, the style of which had last been seen at the Brighton Pavilion circa 1912, with a bathing cap and goggles. Calista wore a tank suit.

"Oh God, I'm jealous!" Rudy said when she had appeared on the beach. "You're so long-waisted. I would be long-waisted, too, if I was taller. Hee-hee," Rudy cackled, splashing water up on the beach. "Come on, sweetheart, in you go. I'm eighty-one years old and skin and bones. If I can take it, you can. It's marvelous for circulation. You know, I have no blood-pressure problems. Thank God—all those old coots who take those blood-pressure medicines can't ever get it up."

"Don't talk dirty, Rudy!" Titty flicked some water toward him.

"Do you do water ballet, Calista?" Rudy asked, swimming over to her.

"I used to in college. As a matter of fact"—she lowered her voice—"forgive me for talking dirty, but we used to call ourselves the Wet Dreams."

Rudy began to laugh so hard, he nearly sank. When he had recovered, he asked Calista to show him some tricks. She remembered something called a back dolphin and another maneuver called a tuck, which she executed most imperfectly. But by Titty's and Rudy's applause, one would have thought she was Esther Williams.

\* \* \*

After the swim, they sat on the porch, wrapped in thick dark green terry-cloth robes monogrammed with frogs intertwined with the letter *N*.

"I like a girl who likes her bourbon," Rudy said as he looked at Calista. He liked Calista. He thought that had he not been born the way he was, this would have been precisely the kind of woman he would have wanted to share his bed with, his life. He liked her sharp wit, her irreverence, and her long, solid legs and hooded dark eyes. Her easy style, too. She was so different from anything he had ever encountered. She was not theatrically bohemian like all those artsy-fartsy Cambridge types so often were. He chuckled to himself when he remembered what that ass Bambi had said after meeting Calista—or had it been Cornelia? They were so interchangeable, those two. But one of them had called her "socially fascinating." What they'd really meant was, How could a Baldwin have become involved with a Jew? "Socially fascinating" was a code for things that were not WASP and Brahmin in Boston. The Kennedys and the late Judge Louis Brandeis were considered "socially fascinating."

Just before dinner, Rudy descended the great staircase in cream-colored knickers and a Norfolk jacket; then Titty followed in something that looked like a well-tailored pup tent with a beautiful nubbly woven shawl. All Calista had brought was jeans. But instead of a sweater, she had brought an old Chanel jacket that belonged to a suit she had picked up in Filene's basement. She decided she'd better wear it, since it was the only slightly dressy thing she had brought. Calista liked odd combinations and this was one. The faded denims actually went rather well, if unexpectedly, with the jacket, which was a white wool the texture of cottage cheese and had the characteristic Chanel braid trim and gold buttons.

"Darling, I adore it," exclaimed Rudy as she appeared in the dining room. "Chanel—you know, I knew her very well. We shared a lover at one time." He studied her. "Would you mind if I suggested one touch? I have just the thing for your neck. You have a lovely neck, but it looks cold sticking out of that collar, and believe me, this room isn't warm."

"Certainly. I forgot to bring a scarf or a turtleneck."

"It's upstairs. Be back in a flash," Rudy said.

"Here, dear." Returning, he held out a silk ascot in a tiny plaid, the most beautiful Calista had ever seen.

"Oh, how elegant." It felt like water between her hands.

"Marvelous texture, isn't it? Woven from English silk rep, mills in East Anglia. That is where all the best silk for ties comes from."

"The colors!" marveled Calista.

"Yes, such clarity. You see, that is because the weft is floated on the surface of the material instead of being woven in."

"I've never seen this plaid."

"Well, it's actually popularly known as the Prince of Wales check. Look closely and you'll see it's a very fine grain over-check printed on a Glen Urquat plaid. But there's a departure in the usual colors. These, I would call a custard and rhubarb."

In the dining room, one end of the long wooden-planked table had been set with three plates—all emblazoned with the Nohq-wha logo of an *N* intertwined with frogs. There was a small fire crackling in the huge fireplace that was built from cyclopean rocks. Candles on a massive chandelier over the table had been lighted. Dinner was served by Hoops and observed by a half dozen elk heads mounted on the wall. It was simple: roast chicken, wild rice, sugar snap peas, salad, and apple pie. After dinner, they moved to the built-in bench seats by the fire. There was a chaise of peeled poles polished with beeswax and heavily cushioned for Titty. Then it was brandy and soda for Titty and Rudy and soda without brandy for Calista; for indeed, she felt as smooth and relaxed as the English silk rep and did not want to deal with the headache brandy often gave her. A few yawns, some vague references to an early-morning swim, and then good nights all around. It was perfect.

# 16

She slept with the shutter slats open so the chilly air and the spruce scent could come through the window. She used the extra blanket and wore socks to bed. As soon as her head hit the pillow, Calista fell asleep.

When the first gray light of morning seeped through the open slats, she awoke. Alert, refreshed, and—who knew—possibly ready for that early-morning swim. When she looked at her watch, she saw that it was only five o'clock. She felt restless after just two pages of *Barchester Towers* and one absurdly treacly poem of Rupert Brooke's about an old love.

She looked around the room that had been Muffy's and wondered whether she had been like Bootsie. It suddenly occurred to Calista that perhaps there were other artifacts and mementos of Muffy's aside from the Rupert Brooke book with the pressed corsage. The notion of this was enough to get her to an upright position in the bed. She looked about. There were half a dozen little built-in cupboards and an odd-shaped closet in the corner under the eaves, with the top of its door slashed off at an angle. Why not explore? She swung her legs out from under the covers.

The first built-in was empty; the second had a dead mouse and some old tennis shoes; the third, a stack of old newspapers. She took them out and found ferns pressed between the pages of a *Boston Evening Transcript,* a paper long expired. She went over to the small closet, which looked as if it had been built for dwarfs. It was quite dark. On the floor, there was a large cardboard box. She pulled it out. In faded gold scroll was the name Priscilla's of Boston. Of course, Priscilla's was the famous Newbury Street wedding-dress couturier. Brides and debutantes were her clients. Muffy and probably Bambi had bought their gowns for these major events from Priscilla. Calista doubted, however, that a wedding dress was in the box. She slid her fingers under the edges of the top and lifted it. "Oh!" she gasped.

Her first instinct was actually to put the lid right back on. There was this sense of trespassing. She knew, in that instant, as she looked down on the handless drawing, that she was approaching an edge, an abyss, and within that abyss there was a terrible secret, a secret that had devoured, a truth that had killed.

But should she look? She was becoming a trespasser in the darkest woods of a shadowed mind. She slid the picture over. There was another, and another. All three were very similar to the ones she had seen in the hallway off of the Kingsleys' pantry on Louisburg Square. But it was the fourth one that made her blink. The background was black, with bars of white falling across in rhythmic intervals. Then descending from the top of the paper were three pendulous pink shapes. Calista looked across the room. Slats of light fell through the shutter, across the bed, and onto the floor in an identical pattern to the ones in the picture. This would be the child's view, and of course the child would try not to focus on the swinging pink genitalia, but . . . She raised her hand to cover her mouth, to hide a secret, to say "Sshhh!" Her hands trembled as she set the drawing down on the floor. There were dozens of slat drawings.

She hadn't even heard the door open, but the slats of light on the wood floor were suddenly cut by a clawed shadow.

The voice was terrible. It was thick, deep, and barely human. "You guessed. I knew you would." Titty loomed above Calista—immense and dark, her eyes cold reptilian slits.

# 17

Leon Mauritz groaned and drummed his fingers on the inlaid edge of his desk. "What do you mean that the nose was chopped off in the same way? Be precise. You mean it was the same tool as used on the kouros at the Met?" He paused and listened, then resumed. "This is an honest error that anyone could have made. The problem is that you shouldn't have touched it in the first place, given the talk. . . . Yes . . . yes . . . I know. . . . Well, the infrared studies should help with that. . . . Yes, dear. Look at that thing in Indianapolis with the mosaics . . . that's infinitely worse, and it was financed by a bank. The woman was strictly an amateur. Yes, yes, I know . . . yes . . . well, don't. Life's too short. Okay . . . good-bye, dear."

Mauritz hung up the phone and sighed deeply. He was not a therapist. He was a consultant and sometime dealer in antiquities. It wasn't his fault that the Getty had walked into it with the damn kouros figure. It really had been stupid for them even to look at that statue, because there had been a whiff about it for years. And now the new technology for sniffing out these whiffs of fraud was proving about as reliable as the Bible, at least in the case of the dubious origins of the kouros. Quote any Scripture you want and prove your point. So much for science here. It was very difficult to pin anything down with these marbles of the fifth and sixth centuries. It wasn't like paintings, where pigments and techniques, as well as paper and canvas, had varied distinctly over the years. Stone was stone. The phone rang again. God, it was Saturday, and naturally, Griselda his secretary wasn't in. He hesitated. He just had a sense before he picked it up that this next call would also not be an altogether-pleasant one.

"Hello." The voice was unnaturally high-pitched. "Mr. Mauritz?"

It was Madame X, as he had come to think of her, for she would not reveal her name. "I was able to obtain the second netsuke."

"But I thought you were not interested in selling."

"I am not interested now. But at a later date perhaps, and I felt you might get me in contact with such collectors at that time. I mean you've been so helpful thus far."

"Well, you hope I have been."

There was a pause. "What do you mean?"

"Well, frankly, madame, I usually don't deal in this way. It is highly irregular for a person to call up, insist on anonymity—at least to this degree—and then only verbally describe the object over the phone. If the first netsuke is indeed as you have described—but I can never be sure of that without seeing it, or at least photographs—but if it is as you describe, then I say it is worth something, if you have its mate. It is the pair that counts; separately, they are nothing."

"Yes, yes. I understand."

"So I will not at this point give you any contacts."

"Would you hazard a guess as to what the pair might be worth?"

Mauritz closed his eyes. There was a joke among Jews. It seemed applicable now. "Please God," prayed the old Jew from the shtetl that had just been wasted by the czar, "next time, choose someone else." "Well, Madame," Mauritz continued, "if indeed these are the signed Tomotados, genuinely signed Tomotados, I would think they would fetch together one million dollars."

"Thank you. I'll be in touch."

Leon Mauritz stared at the phone. He didn't like this business with the netsuke at all. It reeked. He wondered where the call had come from. Possibly New York or San Francisco; more likely, Boston. There were small cadres of people in Boston who were gaga over Asian art. Most of them tended toward the awful China Trade stuff—Canton and lacquer *tsatskes.* It might have been worth a call to Archie Baldwin or the inimitable Jack Thayer, both scions of Boston Puritan princes. But Archie was in some jungle, God knew where, and dear Jack had died two years before—a death that almost palpably impoverished the world that knew him. There was, of course, Rudy Kingsley.

Rudy had been Mauritz's first "older man." The affair had been brief but satisfying. And they had remained friends. Rudy had taught him as much as anybody about Greek antiquities. Indeed, the first whiffs on the kouros had been wafted by Rudy. When was that? Back in the late fifties. God, time flies. Now he was practically the age Rudy had been at that time. Well, it was irrelevant, because Rudy was in England. He planned to go over in September. He might mention it if he had time to get down to Oscar House. In the meantime, he was feeling quite depressed and he had yet another funeral to go to for a young art dealer who had succumbed to the dread disease.

# 18

"I told Rudy that I knew you would," Titty was saying. Calista's whole rib cage seemed to shake with the thundering of her heart. She was down on the floor, looking at the drawings. This woman could easily crack her on the head with that pronged cane. She had to play for time.

"I guessed what, Titty?"

"Well, about Muffy, of course, and what he did to her and to Boots, I'm sure. It runs in the family, don't you know?" She suddenly appeared terribly tired. The color had drained from her face. She looked absolutely gray, like an immense, wrinkled Hubbard squash. Calista looked down at the drawings of the slats of white against the dark with the pendulous pink loops. "You mean"—she spoke quietly, her voice barely audible—"he raped her and Bootsie?"

"Yes." Then the tiny voice seemed absolutely strangled. Great tears rolled out of the slitted eyes.

"And you, too?"

"Oh no, not Kingie. His father, Tad."

"He raped you?"

Titty nodded, her chin quivering.

"Did you tell anybody?"

"Only Rudy. See, Rudy had suspected because he had an older sister. She had died here one summer. She was just twelve or thirteen at the time. But Rudy had suspected that he had done something—you know what I mean—to Sassy. He used to hear cries and whimpers. But she would never say anything."

"So did you and Rudy tell your parents?"

"No. You see, first of all, we were the poor relatives—only here by the grace of Tad and Abigail. They handed over the land and built the house for us. It was one of those dollar-a-year things. And my parents would never have believed it. They thought Tad was God."

"Couldn't Rudy have told them?"

"Yes, I have been asking myself that for—what, seventy years now?" Rudy stood in the door in a silk dressing gown and velvet slippers, looking frail as a leaf. "I finally did tell them, but it was too late."

Titty looked up at Rudy. "She figured it out, dear. I knew she would." He came in and sat down on the bed by Titty and put an arm around her shoulders.

"Just from these pictures, you figured it out, my dear?"

"I'm not sure," Calista said honestly. Had she figured out what she thought, or had they thought she had figured out murder? "I really don't know how it happened. I guess I first started thinking that something might be wrong when I saw the handless pictures in the pantry at Quintana's, the ones Bootsie and Muffy drew."

"Handless pictures?" Titty said vaguely.

"Yes, like these." Calista shuffled back through the pictures on the floor and held one up. "See."

"Oh yes, I see!" Titty said, leaning forward with intense interest. "These are just like the ones I drew in Dr. Schlemmer's office in Vienna."

"Dr. Schlemmer . . . Vienna?"

Rudy now spoke. "Yes, you see when Titty was about twenty,

she had a complete nervous breakdown. Her parents sent her to Switzerland to some ridiculous hospital where they gave you mud baths and laudanum—that was basically the therapy."

"And sleeping," Titty added. "Sleeping was a big part of it."

"Well, it was ridiculous. Then when I heard them making sounds about a lobotomy, I was just horrified. Freud by now had a wide reputation, and I knew someone who had studied with an associate of Freud's, Wolfgang Schlemmer. I hustled Titty right out of that Swiss joint and down to Vienna to be psychoanalyzed."

"He was wonderful," Titty said. "You never heal from something like this, but you find out ways to go on living. You discover that there is more to life than being a victim. That's the most important part. You learn how not to be a victim. Dr. Schlemmer did that for me."

"But I just can't believe it," Calista was saying, and even while she was saying it, she knew it sounded dumb. Everyday there were articles in the paper about abused children. "And you say it runs in the family?"

"Oh absolutely," Rudy said. "In an odd way, it is probably why I am a homosexual."

"What do you mean? Were you abused?"

"Oh no, not sexually abused. I am gay for a lot healthier reasons than that. But you see, you must know about America and particularly Boston of that time. If you read the nineteenth-century historians, you will come to see that American males felt they were the most male creatures on earth. How this translated in terms of the young males of lineage in Boston meant that not only were they superb sportsmen, played games, knew how to drink, and had some inclination toward scholarship but it was all bound up with class and the Brahmin sense of stewardship. You eschewed ostentation and lavish expenditure, for instance; it was not only inappropriate in the Puritan sense; it was slightly foppish. You avoided atmospheres of money like Bar Harbor or Newport, for example. It was not considered fit or socially responsible for people of advantage to flaunt it in such ways as they did in New York. Embedded at the center of all of these notions was an archetype of masculine behavior. You went to the frontier, like Parkman. You explored the Arctic perhaps; as a boy, you read *Robinson Crusoe* and *Two Years Before the Mast.* You supported the arts, but you did not become an artist. You might have salons for artistic types, but you did not sleep with them or let them borrow money. At a certain point, usually by November of your freshman year at Harvard, you were taken to a reputable brothel—there was one in Quincy—where you were initiated into the mysteries of sex, which you came away from totally underwhelmed and perhaps slightly embarrassed. After that, you visited the brothel infrequently and found Irish girls clerking downtown in department stores with whom you could try out your sexual skills for free. Parsimony being a virtue, of course. Then you retreated to places like Nohqwha for bracing masculine weekends of blood sports. This was all considered the essence of manliness in Boston, because all this was done properly by proper Bostonians in the Hub, and it was around the Hub that the earth revolved; for although Rome might be the Eternal City, it was Boston that was the center of the universe. And its men were responsible for maintaining the torque that kept the Hub revolving.

"That, of course, was a very narrow definition of virility as far as I was concerned—a xenophobic version, in fact. I didn't consider it manly at all. I hated this cultish worship of Parkman. I hated their blood sports. That's why I always wear bright colors and red braces in the country. I want to alert the animals: 'I'm here. Run! . . .' Not that I'd shoot any of them, ever. I hated their stupid games. I loved beautiful objects. I loved the classical nude sculptures. They aroused me, yes, but I loved them for what they said about men during a golden era in civilization. And I loved the love between men. I always hated that psalm that said 'The Lord delighteth not in any man's legs.' My rationale for that is that God's a woman and she's lesbian. So now you ask, Was I sexually abused for my attitude? No. But my father loathed me. He couldn't believe I was the way I was. I was a blight on everything he valued. He hated me as a child dressing up in my togas and running around in the woods up here. Oh, it was fine for the men on their manly retreats to go swimming nude, but let me show up with a bedsheet I had fashioned into a toga and with a wreath of birch leaves on my head and it was as if I had marched stark naked into a waltz evening in Boston and pulled Mr. Hooper's dong.

"I suppose, however, being a total outcast within one's own family constitutes some kind of abuse. In any case, my father certainly was not going to let this kind of thing happen with Kingie, although Kingie was older and had none of my 'tendencies.' But father decided to imbue him double strength with all that virility, to give him the manliness that I lacked, in addition to his own. I know that Kingie knew what was happening in that bedroom with Sassy, and I am almost sure that Kingie became part of the abuse. It was his initiation into manly pleasures—try it out on your sister."

Calista felt almost numb. "So it is a tradition."

"Yes," said Titty.

Rudy sighed and crossed his legs. "Well, let's say that they never thought of it as an aberration, a pathology. My homosexuality yes, but having intercourse with a daughter or a niece—no. But in the final analysis, yes, it became a tradition. It was very easy for Kingie to carry on with it. You must understand that we are families steeped in tradition. So anything that has been done before in this sense has a patina of rightness about it. It is condoned."

"It's sick," said Calista.

"But it's tradition. They worship tradition."

"But what about the women? Didn't they suspect? Didn't they do anything about it?"

"I honestly don't think my mother suspected," Titty was saying. "And if she had, I don't think she or my father had the imagination to know what to have done. They felt beholden to Tad and Abigail. But it would never have gotten that far. They were experts at denial. They raised it to an art form in all matters."

"But what about Abigail? Your mother, Rudy?"

"What about Abigail?" he said with contempt. "It is true she never knew, until I told her."

"So you did finally tell her?"

"Yes. When the talk began years later about the lobotomy. I was furious. Almost murderous, to tell you the truth, and I blurted it all out. I suggested that rather than a lobotomy for Titty, how about castration for Tad. That was the last I saw of either of my parents. They cut me from their wills."

"They did?" Calista's eyes widened. Rudy nodded. "Then how did you make all this money?"

"Well, I had already come into part of my trust fund by my twenty-first birthday and had doubled that. They also couldn't touch the money that my grandmother Eloise had set aside for me. I was a favorite of Eloise's and, although I am not sure she was ever told the entire story of my disinheritance, I always had the oddest sense that she knew all about the circumstances. Even beyond that, I began to wonder if my grandfather's death was in reality the suicide they claimed it to be. I was not the first to wonder if he had not been helped along. It was shortly after he and Eloise had separated."

"Separated?" Calista said. "Wasn't that unusual for those times?"

"Divorce was unusual, but not separation. As I have grown older and with the benefit of emotional distance, I have concluded that this tragic tradition of abuse began with my grandfather Theodore, and—who knows—possibly before. But Eloise, my grandmother, was the only woman to ever do anything about it. There had been a daughter, Marella, whom she had suddenly, and for no apparent reason, whisked out of the house and out of Boston. They went to Paris and then to Florence to live together. They became part of that circle of American expatriots toward the end of the last century. It was an interesting group. John Singer Sargent and his family were part of it. You know, Sargent was born in Florence. Of course, Eloise had a lot more money than the Sargents. But they would traipse about to the various spas and cities in a strange nomadic existence. Marella and John Singer became quite close. I even think she entered the atelier of Carolus-Duran with him in the 1870s in Paris. And Marella willed to me two Sargents, which are now in the Philadelphia Museum of Fine Arts. But back to the story. Marella became the heir not only to two Sargents but to the lion's share of grandfather Theodore's estate. It was disproportionately large, her share in comparison to Tad's. You can bet this was Eloise's doing. Eloise was very cunning. It was after one of her trips back to the States that grandfather Theodore was found dead of a self-inflicted gunshot wound. Blew his head off with a duck-hunting gun—that is the weapon of choice among our kind for suicide. Samuel Warren used a duck gun, too."

Calista was absolutely dizzy with all that Rudy and Titty had been telling her for the last twenty minutes. She looked down at the drawings again and then picked up another piece of paper on which something was scrawled. "What about Queenie? Did she know what was going on?"

"I'm sure. But again, she would deny on a very deep level. I do remember once when they came over to England, Queenie and the girls, Muffy and Bootsie. They visited me and then I took them on a wonderful trip through the Hebrides and the Orkneys. Queenie never said a word to me about anything specific. But there was this feeling of putting something behind, of fresh starts. As a matter of fact, she was very interested in grandmother Eloise and at one point I think we toyed with the idea of going over to see Marella in Paris. She was very old at that time, however. She lived to be well over one hundred."

Calista picked up the piece of paper she had been holding and looked at it more carefully. It was in the wobbly hand of a child just learning to write cursive.

"What's that?" Titty asked, leaning forward to get a better look.

"I'm not sure," Calista said. "A poem maybe."

"What does it say?" Titty asked.

" 'Little Mother, Little Mother,' " Calista began to read.

" 'Gone away, gone away. Away, away I float. Leave just those parts behind. From the cage with bars of moonlight, bars of sunlight, I fly on my wings unbroken.' "

Titty had raised her hand to her mouth as if to stifle a cry. "That's what Kingie used to call Muffy, 'Little Mother.' It made my skin crawl. It was when I first heard him call her that that I began to suspect. I should have done something. But I didn't know what to do. That . . . that poem . . ." Titty pointed a plump, shaky finger at the paper. "That describes it perfectly. You see that is exactly what you do. You float out of your body. You take your brain and leave the rest behind. You imagine you're elsewhere, anywhere else but where you are. You teach yourself to endure, not to protect yourself, but just to get through it. If there is one thing an abused child learns how to do, it is to be abused. You become nothing more than a vagina. But your mind is somewhere else all the time."

"This is horrible. Just too horrible. And Queenie just let it happen?"

"Yes," said Rudy quietly. "She would never risk facing it. She would never risk divorce. She was a very conventional person, you know. She had made, after all, what was considered to be a superb marriage by all counts. And that was what determined a woman's fate in Boston of that era."

"But her children?"

"They suffer, and if they don't die from it, they begin to hate. Bootsie did hate her mother. I hated Aunt Abigail almost more than Uncle Tad."

"What happened to Muffy? Did she hate, too?"

"Of course. She hated most of all. The only way she could kill the big mother was to kill the Little Mother." And Calista saw hate swell in Titty's face.

They took a walk, then took a swim. Titty gathered some wildflowers. They did all the things that one was supposed to do at a summer place. But it all had changed from yesterday. It was as if there was a presence. The island, the woods, the house was full of little ghost girls fleeing, screeching in their silent terror as they were invaded, penetrated. This was where childhood had been slaughtered—at Nohqwha.

They returned to the house to pack up their things and go back to Boston. Calista heard the phone ring outside the bedroom as she was packing. A minute later, Rudy appeared at her door.

"A new development," he said. Titty was just coming down the hall.

"About Quintana?"

"Yes, a possible motive."

"What?" Calista and Titty both asked.

"Apparently, something is missing. Two priceless netsukes are gone."

"Netsukes?" Calista repeated.

"Yes. The toggle worn on the Japanese sash, the obi, by which the obi cord could be tied up and secured. Some are quite valuable and there are people throughout the world who collect netsukes quite passionately."

"But . . . but . . ." Titty stammered. "The police said nothing was missing, and Boots and Gus didn't think anything was, either."

"Well, they are quite small. They might have just overlooked them. Boots and Gus were in no state, of course, at that time to be taking detailed inventories."

"Yes, yes. Something that small is easy to overlook," Titty said.

Unless, of course, Calista thought, one was a connoisseur of Asian art and knew what to look for first. It was almost as if Rudy was reading Calista's mind.

"Of course, they might not be of any real value at all." A nervous shadow flickered across his face.

## 19

"So you don't have a father?" Jamie stared hard into his sand-wich with a concentration it did not require.

"No, he's dead. Why did you ask?"

"Oh, I don't know. I just kind of wondered."

Kind of wondered my ass, Charley thought. This was the first vaguely personal thing this kid had ever said to him. The kid was a total zombie. Charley regretted the day he had ever met him, let alone told him about the opening on the swan boats. But he was caught in this terrible bind. This kid seemed irreparably dam-aged to Charley and he couldn't put his finger on it.

"You got a father?" Charley asked.

"Not around."

"Where is he?"

"California. He's got a new wife and new kids—brand-new everything." Jamie laughed bitterly. Yeah, thought Charley, they are all brand-new and you really are damaged old goods, aren't you?

"You ever go see him?"

"Naw . . . uh . . . he comes here sometimes."

"So it's just you and your mom." Charley decided to be bold.

"Yeah . . . yeah, just me and Mom."

"Well, that's almost the same as me. Me and my mom, except when Archie's around."

"Who's Archie?"

"My mom's friend—like boyfriend."

"They sleep together?"

"Yeah."

"Is that like weird for you? I mean, you know, like him not being your dad or stepdad."

"Naw. I mean it's not like she's had this string of boyfriends revolving through her bedroom. At least Archie's the only one I know about who's spent the night at our place, and I really like him a whole bunch."

"That's cool."

No, thought Charley, it's not just cool. There's something more going on here with Jamie. He was going to push it. "I guess, you know, maybe it is kind of weird thinking about your parents or your mom doing it . . . sex, I mean."

Jamie got up quickly and brushed off his pants. "I wouldn't know. My mom's too tanked most of the time to do much of anything." He laughed again and headed back toward the swan boats.

A filigreed shadow played across Titty's jowls, which rested comfortably in the nest of pearls encircling her throat. She was squashed into a wing chair with a teacup and saucer poised above her formidable bosom. "In the middle of August, there is no more discreet place than the Athenaeum. And I have always sought discretion," she said cryptically. "It's all part and parcel of the syndrome, so to speak."

Every Wednesday, tea was served at the private library, and Titty had called Calista to join her. Calista was familiar with the Athenaeum and had often used it for research. It had proved particularly helpful for tracking down some of the original Robin

Hood source material when she was working on *Marian's Tale.* It was the most august of Brahmin settings, with its marble busts gazing down from lofty niches, its neoclassical detailing and soaring Palladian windows. Calista was intimately familiar with the moldings throughout the library. They were the most exquisite in Boston and she had done painstaking sketches of them for the palace of the Beast, in *Beauty and the Beast,* a story that she had avoided illustrating for years because she was so terribly uncomfortable with its sexuality. However, once she had decided on the neoclassical motif with a decidedly pre-Raphaelite look to the landscape and characters, she had been more comfortable. It struck her as very odd now that here of all places, the Boston Athenaeum, she was discussing incest with a descendant of one of the most revered families of the Commonwealth. For although Titty's parents had not been nearly as wealthy as the Kingsleys or the Parkingtons, their lineage was equally dazzling and had its fair share of Adamses and Cabots and indeed Reveres and Brattles. Now Titty was telling her a horrific story about a trip to Newport when she was just fourteen or fifteen.

"Yes, we usually went down there for a week every summer, although Newport was somewhat frowned upon by many Bostonians. It was really a New York place. Vanderbilts, you know, that ostentatious crowd. But anyhow, both through my parents and Rudy's, we had relatives there. They gave the most lavish parties. The great flower of Newport was the American Beauty rose. Everyone grew them in those garish gardens they favored down there. You know, those homes were really in such bad taste. Big piles of pink Italianate stucco. In any case, every Newport hostess would try to outdo the others. They all loved splendor and they devoted their lives to creating it—chandeliers with crystal drops the size of oranges; everything overdone, overripe. There was one party where the host hung fourteen-karat-gold fruit from the branches of all the trees in the garden to create a *bois doré.* At another party, servants dressed as water nymphs, mermaids, and Tritons swam in blue-tiled pools; they would rise up dripping from the pools and offer bowls of fruit to the guests. But as I was saying, the American Beauty rose—well, Newport felt it had an imprimatur on that flower. So it was always part of some party motif. And it certainly was the main theme at a Vanderbilt ball the year I was first allowed to attend. Five other young lovely girls and myself were to be part of the decor."

Calista visibly winced. "Yes, dear, I know. This was way before women's lib." Titty took a sip of her tea and continued. "Well, we were led in wearing our lovely white gowns with satin ribbons wrapped round our wrists. It was supposed to be a kind of daisy chain, I suppose. Or rather, a rose chain, for we were then tethered, each of us to a rosebush."

"Oh how awful!" exclaimed Calista.

"You have no idea how awful, especially if you had been violated as I had for the previous five or six years. I felt as if I was a stain on this beautiful tableau; that I didn't belong in the company of these pure, flawless creatures in their white gowns; that I must have stuck out like a sore thumb; that my terrible secret must show. You see, that is the most awful thing. Ever since Tad had begun doing these horrible things to me, I felt that although it was a dreadful secret, everyone knew or suspected and that they blamed me. Even the fireflies on the screens knew my terrible secret; they were the same fireflies that were on the screens in the boathouse where Uncle Tad often took me. But worst of all was the feeling that in some strange way Uncle Tad had given his permission for other men to treat me this way. It was confirmed on that night at the Vanderbilt ball. A cousin of Tad's, one I had never met from Connecticut . . ." Titty's voice dwindled off.

Calista reached forward and took Titty's hand. "I was so angry," Titty continued. "I was desperate, and Rudy wasn't there. But I was sure that Aunt Abigail knew about it. I was just sure. And she was happy that it was this cousin and not her husband, Tad, this time. I could have killed her. So I can understand now how maybe"—Titty's voice dropped very low—"Bootsie could have perhaps murdered Queenie . . . but we must protect her no matter what."

"It doesn't look good with this netsuke theft . . . but then again, it seems so . . . so . . ."

"So what?"

"Obvious, I guess. I mean, Bootsie is the one who knows Asian art in the family, the one who has the connections."

"Not necessarily. Diggory and his sister-in-law Cornelia know a thing or two. They collect scrolls, I believe."

"But they're so old. And they certainly don't need the money. Does Bootsie?"

"I have no idea what Boots's financial condition is. She must get something from her former husband. I know that Rudy has given her some stock. But that's Rudy, forever generous."

"What about Gus? Has he given any to Gus?"

"I would imagine. Gus can't make much on that prep school teaching salary." Titty paused. "You know, perhaps I shouldn't say this, but Rudy always suspected that Gus might have tendencies."

"Tendencies?" Calista asked.

"You know—homosexual—gay, as they call it."

"Gus?" Calista's eyes widened in surprise.

"Oh nothing overt like Rudy. Good Lord, Kingie would have killed him if he had ever given the slightest hint. It's just a feeling that Rudy has had for a long time."

"Well actually, that might be a relief, considering the family history of heterosexual abuse of young girls."

"Yes, yes, I always thought so," Titty said primly.

# 20

As Charley pedaled the swan boat to the dock, he noticed the dapper little man in a blue blazer with a crest on the pocket and a cap on his head. He looked like an illustration from one of his mom's children's books. He looked familiar, too. It dawned on Charley as he was stepping aboard who the little man was. The man managed to get into the last row of benches, the one directly ahead of the swan seat where Charley sat between the two large wings and pedaled.

"Charley Jacobs," the man said, and turned around on the bench, offering his hand. "Rudy Kingsley, a friend of your mother's."

"Yeah, I know. What are you doing here?"

"You bear a striking resemblance to your mother. It's the coloring, I think, and the shape of the eyes. Yes, that's it." The boat was almost fully loaded and the attendants on the pier had begun to shove it along manually. Charley began pedaling. A grandmother and her granddaughter had taken the seat next to Rudy. "I always say a trip to Boston is not complete without a swan-boat ride," Rudy said expansively. "Except, of course, if it is winter. Here, madame." He spoke to the woman next to him. "I happen to have bought some extra peanuts. Would the little girl like to feed the ducks?" They were most appreciative and soon became engaged in the feeding activity. Rudy then turned to Charley.

"I have arranged with the head boatman back there, or whoever that person is who seems to be directing things, for you to take an extended lunch hour tomorrow. You do own a jacket and tie, I presume?"

"Yes, sir."

"Wear it. Meet me at Locke-Ober's at twelve-fifteen. I'll be upstairs in the Ober Room, at the table in the northeast corner. It's my table."

"Northeast," Charley said vaguely.

"Take a compass if it's a problem. They do still teach geography, don't they?"

"Oh yeah, sure."

"Jock, the maître d' will be on the lookout. And by the way, don't mention anything to your mother about this—just yet."

Charley leaned forward a bit and pedaled harder as they were circling the duck island. "What's this all about, sir, the lunch and all?"

Rudy turned around. His face had a look of puckish delight. The minnow eyebrows leapt toward the neat brim of his cap and his lips moved around each letter of the word elastically. However, no one would have ever suspected the word this extremely effeminate dapper little gent was spelling. It was *M-U-R-D-E-R.*

"Look at him. Wasn't he beautiful?" Titty said, pointing to a faded photograph of Rudy at about the age of ten or eleven. Calista and Titty had taken a cab back to Titty's duplex on the corner of Dartmouth and Commonwealth Avenue. The apartment had a bewildering array of the detritus of over a century of New England materialism. To the untutored eye, it appeared to be a confusing collection of stuff, which, although seemingly unconnected, did have a kind of pattern that could have spoken only of the inclinations of merchant princes and Puritans.

China pug dogs stood sentry duty beneath an elaborately carved mantel. A vermilion Japanese fan filled the fireplace. There were vitrines displaying porcelain shepherdesses and willowware side by side, as if in defiance of any dictums charging that never the twain shall meet. Shawls were draped across the backs of love seats. Legions of tufted and tasseled footstools were scattered about as if awaiting Titty's swollen feet at anyplace she might decide to sit. Embroidered cushions and Oriental rugs were everywhere. An immense silver service stood on a sideboard. The service involved tiered trays supported by drooling silver greyhounds. Calista looked up from the photo album, her gaze falling upon the dogs. Titty observed her.

" 'Majestic bad taste,' that's what Rudy calls that thing. To tell you the truth, I don't know how it wound up here. It did come down through my mother's side of the family, presumably before they lost all their money in the crash of '73. You know, the Crédit Mobilier and all that." Calista's American history was shaky, but Crédit Mobilier did ring a dim bell. "I would think," Titty continued, "it would be worth more than those netsuke things taken from Queenie's. My God, if you'd melt that thing down . . . well, maybe I should." Titty giggled. "It's hell to dust. Be worth more as silver bars."

"Oh look! There's a picture of me and Rudy. I think I'm Diana the huntress," Titty said, pointing to another photograph in the album she had open on her lap. There was a photo with curling edges of two somber-looking children swathed in sheets. Titty had dark curls and was carrying a bow. "I think those were my mother's furs draped over my shoulder." Calista turned the page. She felt something quicken.

"Oh dear," said Titty, "these are really out of order."

Calista bent closer. "What in the world?" she whispered. There was something very strange, very wrong about the picture.

"That's the Welles Club 'Frivolities,' my dear. When the gents dress up like women—or tarts."

"They don't even look human," Calista said in a soft voice. Titty reached for a magnifying glass. "Let's see. The date on this is 1924. Goodness, I wonder why I'd have this picture. I guess my father must be in it. Ah yes! There he is. Uncle Tad's not in this, but there's Kingie looking quite lissome."

It was all true what Rudy had said about this penchant for dressing up being ultimately a mockery. There was an element of something downright despicable in this picture. The grotesquely painted faces, the hips thrust out to the side, the corsets and fishnet stockings, the snickering expressions. But there was something else, something terribly disturbing about the picture independent of the smirking mockery. It triggered a vague response in Calista's brain, some image, some dim memory, some fragment of a picture, shard of a half-understood dream. What was it? She stared hard at the picture. "That's Kingie?" she asked.

"Yes. Quite handsome, wasn't he? Looked a lot like Rudy, but taller. He wore that corset well, what with his hourglass waist. All of the Kingsleys really cut such marvelous figures. Rudy didn't get their height, but you saw him in his bathing costume."

"Yes, very svelte," Calista said.

"Too bad I didn't get any of the svelte genes." Titty laughed.

But Calista wasn't really hearing her. She was lost in a maze of half images, shreds and slips of thoughts, but nothing would come together. She had to see Bootsie again. Surely she could go over on the pretense of something about Jamie and Charley and the swan boats.

# 21

Calista had been scouring the old soapstone plank in the counter by the kitchen sink for well over five minutes.

"Mom, I think that's clean by now," Charley said.

"Oh . . . yeah, I kind of forgot."

"Forgot what? You seem a little spacey." I am a little spacey, Calista thought. For days, she had been wrestling with whether to tell Charley about her midnight visit to the Kingsleys' greenhouse where, hiding behind the fertilizer bags, she had seen the woman. It had been bad enough trying to figure out what to do before she went to Nohqwha, but now with the discovery of the missing netsukes, it was worse. She had possibly witnessed a crime and not just an intruder. When the woman had stopped to fix her stocking, she had a bag, and in that bag could have been the netsukes.

"I got a problem, Charley," Calista suddenly blurted out.

"What?" Charley asked.

"Hold on a minute." Calista ran upstairs. When she returned, she unfolded a handkerchief on the kitchen table.

"What is that?" Charley said, staring down.

"It's a garter. You know, for ladies stockings."

"Oh. Oh yeah." There was a slight blush that crept across Charley's face. Not that he was such a prude. But as Calista had suspected, Charley had probably looked at some magazines with pictures of women in garter belts, something beyond the Victoria's Secret catalog. "So?"

"So." Calista sighed and began to tell him the story of how she and the garter had crossed paths in the Kingsleys' greenhouse.

When she had finished, Charley looked steadily at her. The gray eyes acquired that strangely luminous quality, so like Tom's, which on others might suggest that all the circuits were down, but Charley's, to the contrary, were in high gear. It was their deep-think look. He drummed his fingers on the table in a rapid-fire staccato. "You're right, Mom. You got a problem." Charley was thinking how Rudy had asked him not to say anything to his mother about their meeting the next day for lunch. He wanted to explain things first. But things were getting really complicated. His mom could, in fact, be implicated in this. What was it? Withholding evidence or something? But was it evidence?

"What makes you think that this person was there to steal these Japanese things that night? It doesn't make sense. Why didn't she take them at the time of the murder? Why revisit the scene of the crime? Isn't that more risk?"

"Yeah, yeah . . ." said Calista slowly. "Unless . . ."

"Unless what?"

"I'm not sure." Calista rubbed her forehead and dug her fingers into her brow.

"Don't do that, Mom. It really makes me nervous. I'm always scared that you're going to gouge your eyes out."

"I'm sorry." How did kids like Charley dare criticize their parents for these little habits? One would think that here, old Charley—whose sneakers sometimes smelled so badly that on occasion she had to spray them with Glade, or who thought nothing of wearing jeans that hung in shreds around his knees—could give a little more latitude in reference to certain parental characteristics. "It's just that I keep losing my train of thought. There is just something that is not fitting here."

"Like a person coming back after the big crime to steal something—yes, very illogical. Doesn't fit."

"No, it's more than that." She stopped again and rubbed her brow. To hell with him. "But if it is illogical, why would they do it?"

"Oooh, Mom! That's great. You're thinking mathematically!" Charley said with a burst of enthusiasm. He had just then decided for sure not to tell his mom about his meeting with Rudy until after the fact.

"I am? What do you know!" said Calista, somewhat mystified.

"Yep."

"I thought mathematics was all logic."

"It is . . . but how do you know what logic is until you figure out what is illogical?"

"Oh."

"It's just like Zorn's lemma."

"What?"

"Zorn's lemma. Dad told me about it a long time ago. But when I was doing that independent thing in set theory last semester . . . well, it was a big part of it."

"Lemma, not dilemma?"

"Yeah, lemma. See, Zorn was this really cool guy and he thought up this very basic thing that is fundamental to algebraic structure theory. It sounds real simple. It says that given an infinite number of sets, it is possible to make a new set by choosing one item from each of the other sets. Sounds simple, doesn't it?"

"Not really."

"Oh, yes it does," said Charley dismissively. "That's the elegance of the whole thing. Deceptively simple. It is really the equivalent of the axiom-of-choice set theory, but more ramifications. It cannot be derived from any of the other axioms in mathematics and yet it is totally universal. Cool, huh?"

"Well, if you say so. But I don't understand how Zorn and this"—she held up the garter gingerly—"come together."

"Me, neither. That's sort of the beauty of it. It's one item from a set. A set that we have posited as being illogical. You said yourself, 'If it is illogical, why would they do it?' The set appears to be syncretic, but that is only if you look at it one way. Implicit in your question is why would they do it? This is a kind of lemma-esque proposition."

"Oh, Charley, you've lost me."

"No I haven't, Mom. Your question was mathematically legitimate, even if you were assuming an illogical stance. Look, you keep doing the illogical part and I'll do the logic. We can work this out. And remember this, Mom." He held up his finger, his eyes were burning bright.

"What?"

"There are an infinite number of sets."

"And I'm supposed to find this comforting?"


For mathematicians, infinities were an aphrodisiac. Calista thought of mathematicians as intrepid wanderers in rimless worlds, realms without confines, undaunted by notions of multiple and simultaneous universes. That was Charley. That was Tom. But she was one who needed edges, perimeters. She was bound to a two-dimensional, finite world. She worked in an arena that could be measured in inches. Books that came in trim sizes of nine inches by eleven, or possibly, if she was feeling very expansive, eleven by twelve. But often she worked in much smaller spaces. And within the paper's edges, she sometimes drew borders to limit the universe of the narrative further, to contain her story.

She lay in bed now, thinking about what she and Charley had discussed. Tortuously, she was trying to make the connection that the photograph from the Welles "Frivolities" had triggered. The sets could not be that limitless. If they were, there was no hope. But the limited sets pointed to Bootsie. Bootsie, with a double motive now: Kill the mother who had let the abuse happen;

and, in some kind of ironic revenge, steal the family jewels. *Family jewels*—the term became freighted with dreadful meaning. Despicable families doing heinous things generation upon generation. Yes, it would be enough to make one murderous. She had not yet told Charley about the sexual abuse. It was so sad. Somehow, it seemed sadder than murder. But she would have to tell him sooner or later if his mathematical inquiries were to come together. Charley had said she should stick to the illogical and he'd take care of the logic.

She smiled to herself in the dark. How blessed she was. And then suddenly, she felt a sharp twinge deep, deep in her mind. It was familiar, but it had been a long time since she had missed Tom with that degree of sharpness, fresh as if it were just yesterday that she had heard the awful news of his death. The terrible realization that he was no more. There was again that kind of lurching disbelief that seizes you when you realize that you will never see someone again. Those moments when you catch yourself thinking, Oh I want to tell him that—or, Won't he love this? Had it been all the talk of the mathematics? It was sharp and keen, this kind of missing, and she had not had it in years. The jolting roller-coaster ride of grief had smoothed out, subsided into a kind of overwhelming sense of loss, which seemed duller and less profound. There had been fewer and fewer sharp twinges, no more mistakes of expecting him to come through the door. You knew now. You knew so well now the meaning of *never*. You had grown accustomed to it and you hated yourself for doing just that. But you were accustomed and, what was worse, you realized that life is infinitely shabbier in the long, dull ache of missing. This was terrible. She had never let herself be so self-indulgent. What about Archie? He had been a wonderful lover, companion, and father for Charley. But at this moment, Archie seemed farther away and more abstract than Tom.

# 22

For a second time, Charley found himself getting dressed as he crossed Boston Common. He had premade his tie that morning so he could just slip it on over the oxford-cloth shirt that he had neatly folded in his backpack. He had stepped beneath the fringed shade of a weeping willow to pull off his T-shirt and change into the other shirt. His mom would have died, but people had exposed worse than that in the Public Garden and the Common.

The bells of Park Street Church were just beginning to chime as Charley reached the corner of Tremont and Park. He continued up Tremont for a short block and then cut into Temple Place, a narrow alley that led directly into Winter Place. Over the entrance was an immense lock with a keyhole and scrolled design. The black-mullioned windows that faced the small, narrow street were half-curtained with lace. Charley straightened his tie and went in.

"Mr. Jacobs." An elderly man in a jacket and white bow tie was at his elbow immediately. "Mr. Kingsley is expecting you. This way, please."

Charley had never seen anyplace like this. He'd been to the Ritz a couple of times when his mom's editor, Janet Weiss, or Ethan Thayer, the publisher, came to town, but this was different. There was leather, beautiful wood, sparkling silver, polished brass, and stained glass. All this was reflected in the flash and glint of mirrors. Nothing really fussy, but it was a little intimidating. They went up a set of stairs. The light became dimmer, the draperies heavier, and the carpet thicker. Charley followed the man into a beautiful room of gleaming dark wood with touches of dull gold. Rudy stood up as he approached the table. He was dressed in a cream-colored suit. His bow tie was a pale peach color, with darker checks. In the eternal twilight of the room, Charley couldn't tell, but he thought that Rudy Kingsley might be wearing makeup. Oh well, it takes all kinds, he thought. He shook hands.

"Welcome, dear boy. Have a seat. Hope you don't mind eating up here out of the hubbub. I find it more restful, more discreet for our subject matter. And alas, I really find that eating lobster bisque under Mademoiselle's tits does something to my digestion."

"What?" Charley's eyes widened.

"Oh, of course. This is your first time to Locke's?"

"Yes, sir."

"Well, downstairs in the bar, there is a famous nude painting. For some unknown reason, for generations she has been called Mademoiselle Yvonne. For years, they used it as an excuse not to seat women downstairs. Then there was the famous liberation of the bar back in August of 1970."

"What happened?"

"A woman, a professor from MIT, called up and made a reservation for Dr. So-and-So. She failed to tell them that the Dr. was herself, a woman."

"So they seated her?"

"Absolutely."

"Now, how about a drink for the young man," said Rudy as a waiter arrived.

"Sure."

"I trust you're not taking in these yet?" He nodded at the two glasses lined up one in front of the other, with clear fluid and olives resting on the bottoms. It did seem a curious arrangement to Charley.

After Charley had ordered a Coke and the waiter had left, Rudy leaned forward and whispered. "Martinis! A delight to be anticipated, my dear, when your palate has developed and your innards have already gone to hell. This is the only way to drink martinis, lined up like this. Jack Benny would always drink from the second one first. Do you know why?"

"No."

"Well, he always said the second one goes down so much easier than the first." Rudy leaned back and laughed, his eyes crinkling into mirthful slits. There is something very likable about this weird little man, Charley thought. "But that's not why I do it," Rudy said. He lifted one of the martinis. "Have you ever seen a lovelier liquid in your life? Isn't it like liquid candlelight? And then if you order two of them, you get these lovely reflections and the play of light off the crystal and the gin in a room like this . . . aahh!" Rudy sighed. In a soft voice, he began to recite.

> There is something about a Martini,
> A tingle remarkably pleasant;
> A yellow, a mellow Martini;
> I wish that I had one at present.
> There is something about a Martini,
> Ere the dining and dancing begin,
> And to tell you the truth,
> It is not the vermouth—
> I think that perhaps it's the gin.

"Ogden Nash," he said. "A verse for almost every occasion— except murder, I believe. And that, of course, is why I have invited you to lunch."

* * *

Rudy waited, however, until the waiter had brought a Coke for Charley.

"Now, as I was saying—about Queenie, Quintana Kingsley, my sister-in-law. You have heard, I trust, about the latest development in the case—the theft of the netsukes."

"Yes." Charley felt something turn inside him. Should he tell Rudy Kingsley about his mom's midnight adventure? Of course not, but he hoped that Rudy wouldn't suspect that he was hiding something.

"Your mother tells me that you are quite ingenious with computers."

"Well, I mess around with them."

"She tells me that on occasion—very special occasions—you are most skillful at cracking into systems." A deep red flush began to crawl up Charley's neck and across his face. He felt his pulse quicken. He was no good at small talk.

"Don't call it *crack*. Call it *hack*. Crackers are evil hackers."

"Well, this is certainly not evil. I just want you to browse around, see what's happening."

"Passive monitoring," Charley said. It wasn't a question; it was a statement. "I don't mess anything up."

"Right. I just need some information."

They ordered and then Rudy explained what he needed.

"Hopkins, Bishop and Creeth," Charley said. All those law firms sounded the same. At first, he thought it sounded like his mom's lawyers, Haverford, Phillips and Beame. "You don't by any chance know what kind of system they use?"

"System?" Rudy asked. Just at that moment, a waiter came with their first course. Shrimp cocktail for Charley, lobster bisque for Rudy.

"Operating system for their computers."

"Oh, I have no idea, dear boy."

"It's probably VAX, with a UNIX system. I can find out. A

friend of mine did a lot of work setting up systems for law firms around here. So what am I looking for?"

"Well, basically, information about the Kingsley estate. Young Harley Bishop still does a lot of work for me. So I am in their files—if you need me as camouflage."

"Do you have any documents with you, any paper stuff at all?"

"Oh no, I'm afraid not. It's all back in England in my office there."

"Where are these guys located—the law firm?"

"One Post Office Square. Why, are you planning on walking right in?" Rudy raised an eyebrow in bemusement. "I thought you could do all this over your electronic wires."

"I can. But some preliminary trashing might help."

"Trashing?"

The waiter arrived with their main courses. Charley blinked as the waiter set down Rudy's plate. There was a mound of dark reddish brown stuff with something on top that looked as if it had died.

"Something wrong, Charley?"

"What is that stuff?"

"Roast beef hash with poached eggs on top."

"Oh." What would people think of next? He dug into his chopped sirloin. He had specified to leave off the mushrooms.

# 23

Just as Charley had thought: In an alley behind Post Office Square, there was a loading dock. Two Dumpsters sat side by side at one end. This would probably be fruitless, but one could never tell. The biggest payoffs in terms of this activity came if one trashed the telephone company. Phone phreaks did it all the time. They could get access codes, discarded manuals, old papers containing passwords, whatever might help them in ripping off service from the baby bells. But then the phone companies started shredding documents with a vengeance when they realized what was happening. Phone phreaks were weird; they didn't just enjoy stealing service, gabbing their heads off and messing up switching stations, but, in addition, they absolutely loved to taunt their victims. Their methods in and of themselves, though, were appealing.

Charley did not see anything wrong in going through folk's trash as long as it wasn't to steal or for blackmail. He might get lucky and find some account information. It was so easy. You could do it in broad daylight. He took off his jacket, tie, roughed up his hair, and began muttering. Most likely, he looked like a somewhat cleaner-than-average homeless person looking for returnable cans or edible garbage. Hopkins, Bishop and Creeth did not believe in shredding—at least not phone logs and phone bills. He took handfuls of paper. He had no idea whether any of it would help him, but Charley liked to be thorough. Just as soon as you decided you didn't need something was exactly when you needed it. This was not going to be a phreaking job—at least not so far, but he wasn't going to leave any base uncovered.

Charley rushed home after work. Luckily, his mother wasn't in. He sent E-mail to Liam Phillips, a computer jock for the Martin Institute, a genetic-research outfit where Charley had worked in an intern program one summer. Liam wrote beautiful code for all the wanna-be Nobel laureates at Martin. He had also been the computer consultant to law firms throughout the country, a specialist in programming for lawyers and writing code for time-keeping programs, so every minute increment could be billed and accounted for.

Later that evening, Charley, in the thick heat of the August night, sat naked at a desk in his bedroom at 16 Louisburg Square. He had Eric Clapton's *Unplugged* playing softly on his CD player. Liam had left a one-word message: UNIX.

This would be pig-easy now for Charley. He picked up the phone and dialed a number.

"Mr. Kingsley, please."

"Just one moment, sir."

Charley waited. There was the click. "Yes?"

"Hi. It's me. Can you call up that Harley guy and ask him for a copy of some document—anything. Tell him you want it on disc because you want to send a copy through Internet to your London office."

"Yes."

"Tell him you got a friend at Harvard in the computer lab that can do it for you, but you just want to see it first."

"I have many friends at Harvard."

"Yeah, you got me. And I still got my dad's old access code; so it's not like you're lying. I mean, I am a legal user on the Harvard system."

"I trust, however, that you are not really going to Internet this."

"No, but if we need an excuse, we got it."

# 24

"No . . . no, Gus, I just can't believe it. . . . Yes. Do you mean that? Okay, yes. . . . I mean, it's just so ridiculous. Do you think I should get Jamie out of town? . . . Yes. I guess you're right; that would arouse more suspicion . . . yes, yes, okay. Good-bye."

Bootsie McPhee put down the phone. How had it all gone so wrong? Jamie! Never! How had this happened? Oh God, she needed a drink. But she needed to think, too. Gus had actually said he would help her. Time to let bygones be bygones, he had said. She laughed out loud harshly. Bygones! So that's what he called it. Well, she had little choice. Hadn't it all started out to protect Jamie? Was it so strange now that it was coming round full circle, so to speak, to this? Maybe she should talk with Rudy? But Gus had said not to. Anything was premature at this point. A panic welled up inside her. She could feel it fluttering and hot, pressing inside her rib cage. There was only one thing that could quell it, smooth it out so she could think. She had to be able to think. She went into the kitchen and took the bottle of vodka from the freezer, where she kept it. She poured two inches into a frosted glass and put in three cubes of ice. She set the glass on a small silver tray. A halo of condensation formed on the tray around the base of the glass. She loved that part. Then carefully, she sliced a thin peel of lemon. Bootsie had her rituals. They were important. It was just a question now, as her hands began to shake slicing the lemon, if it was penance or ritual? Was she delaying the pleasure or prolonging the pain? She set down the lemon and the knife and grabbed hold of the countertop. Her face clenched. Tears, the first in years, squeezed from her eyes. How had every fucking thing gone so fucking wrong in her entire fucking life, and now . . . now just when she needed to be strong for Jamie? Gus said he would be right over. He had to help her. He really owed it to her. Now she really needed him. Oh God, how had it come to this? Hurry, Gus, hurry! she prayed. "I am praying to Gus!" she blurted out loud, her voice cracking with astonishment.

The doorbell rang. She didn't bother to wipe her face. What would he expect, after all?

"Oh my goodness!"

"You?" Bootsie gasped, perplexed. What was Calista Jacobs doing on her front doorstep?

"Bootsie, is something wrong?" How stupid, thought Calista. Something was obviously very wrong. "Are you sick? Can I help you?"

"Oh no, no . . . just uh . . . some upsetting news. Come in? Do you need something?"

Well yes, Calista thought, but so much for the whole ruse of just being in the neighborhood—what the hell, she might as well do as she had planned. "I . . . I was just in the neighborhood and thought I'd drop in and say hi. I think it's great that Jamie is working with Charley at the swan boats. He really enjoys Jamie." Was this sounding as hollow and forced to Bootsie as it was to her? This was so stupid. Why had she ever decided to come here? But Calista had begun to see an inexorable course. Just that morning, a homicide detective had paid a call. It was about the recent netsuke theft.

Oh, they were clever. They had never directly mentioned Bootsie's interest in Oriental art, but Calista could read between the lines. And she had a gut feeling about Bootsie. She just couldn't believe that she had murdered, and, in particular, she couldn't believe that even if she had, the motive would be money. There was too much baggage there, and money was not going to make up for the terrible abuses in the past—the abuse by her father, the outright neglect by Quintana of her daughters in their tragic predicament. It added up to hatred, yes. Calista could believe that Bootsie had a deep well of hatred, but she did not believe that it would lead to murder. Those haunting handless pictures were part of her belief. Bootsie was a profoundly incapacitated person; to take up those shears and plunge them into her mother's chest with her own two hands would be beyond her; at least Calista thought so.

Bootsie stood now in front of Calista, swaying slightly, her face blotchy and her eyes vague and unfocused.

"Yes, isn't it wonderful about Jamie. Come in! Come in!" A new animation crept into her voice. "Oh, I am so happy that he and Charley were able to get together. I mean, Jamie has needed something like this." Bootsie was talking a mile a minute. She seemed to be making a spectacular recovery from whatever bad news she had just received. "Jamie was telling me that Charley is quite the computer buff. You know one of my objections to Poulton Academy—that's Jamie's school—is that it's so old guard and locked into such ridiculous traditions that they do very little with computers. I really think that I may have him change next year . . . now that there is no one to object. To hell with Diggory."

Calista could barely keep up with the stream of verbiage issuing forth. "Would you like some coffee? I still have some left from breakfast or tea, or here's a great idea. It's so hot, maybe I'll put some ice in a glass and we can have iced coffee."

"Fabulous!" Calista said. She felt as if she were drowning in the rushing stream of words. She followed Bootsie into the kitchen. Bootsie got a glass out and filled it with ice cubes and poured in the morning's coffee. "Sugar, milk?"

"A little of both would be fine."

"Great," said Bootsie. "I'll just pour mine in here." She took the coffee pot and poured it into a glass on a silver tray that already had ice in it.

They went out to the living room. Calista took a sip of the coffee. She sat directly across from the Japanese scroll that depicted cranes in flight over a waterfall. Muffy's poem came back, shards of it like slivers of glass:

"Little Mother, Little Mother . . . Away, away I float. Leave just those parts behind. From the cage with bars of moonlight, bars of sunlight I fly on my wings unbroken."

Terrible little mothers, Calista thought, mutilated little mothers. Bootsie was rattling on about Jamie—how she felt he would profit from going to just a regular public school, Brookline High. More in touch with the real world. But Calista just kept staring at the cranes in flight. "You like the scroll?" Bootsie asked, finally breaking out of her nonstop talk.

"Yes. It's quite lovely. So tranquil." Would it be possible to segue, as it were, from Japanese scrolls into incest? Calista wondered. She felt desperate for Bootsie. Perhaps if Bootsie could know that someone else knew, someone who cared, someone who could understand her anger and yet know that she would not have murdered . . . But how could Calista do this? She was just an interfering person who had happened to live next door to the scene of a terrible crime. Those pictures . . . could she ask her about the pictures? But if Bootsie had never been able to talk with Rudy or Titty about this, why would she talk to Calista about it?

"Of course, now with the netsukes being stolen, I guess that moves me into the category of prime suspect, doesn't it?"

Calista gasped.

"Don't look so surprised. With my interests and connections, it's natural." Bootsie spoke almost casually.

"But . . . but . . ." stammered Calista. "You said it really wasn't much of an interest."

"I said that?" Bootsie raised her eyebrow.

"I thought you did."

"Well, it's not a career," she said, lifting her glass for a swallow. She held it to her mouth for a moment before drinking and looked over the rim, the celadon eyes cold as ice. "It doesn't pay . . ." She paused. "Unless you get into something like the netsukes."

Calista was speechless. Just then the doorbell rang. "It's my brother. I've been expecting him." Bootsie jumped up.

They were delayed in the entrance hall. Calista heard a low rapid-fire exchange. Then Bootsie and Gus both walked into the living room with expressions of cheerful well-being that looked like pancake makeup applied with a backhoe. Calista felt alarms going off in every part of her brain. Now both of them started talking nonstop about Jamie. Bootsie sat in the wing chair, her head lolling back, her eyes looking slightly feverish while both she and Gus did a red-hot jig of praise for Jamie. They tossed bits and pieces of talk back and forth while Gus paced around the room, behind the chair where Bootsie sat, neither one of them ever making eye contact with each other. But it was as if every word and glance was being directed toward Calista. "Wonderful boy." "Great idea, Brookline Public High." They were God-blessing Charley and the swan boats all over the place. Relentless talk about computers, summer jobs, college boards, extracurricular activities, on and on until Calista wanted to scream, Stop, you idiots! Don't you know that your mother has been murdered and you, Bootsie, are fast becoming a prime suspect? You said as much yourself. Why all this talk about Jamie? Isn't it time to get down to business here?

"Oh, I just remembered—I have to make a call," Gus said suddenly.

"Use this phone right here," Bootsie said, "unless it is private."

"No, not at all. It's just about the coaching schedule. I coach tennis out at Longwood and at St. Bennett's. Very hectic, come summer, with all the tournaments. I've got to call someone from Longwood now."

Bootsie, in the meantime, had brought over a book of nineteenth-century Japanese scroll paintings to show Calista. They were very beautiful. And Bootsie obviously knew her stuff. In the background, she could hear Gus talking. "No . . . no . . . every Tuesday and Thursday, I'm occupied out at St. Bennett's. It's the only time we can get court time. So I always just spend the night out there in a dorm. It's hardly worth the trip back into Boston. Yeah, yeah. Sorry, Dan, but that's the schedule."

By the time Calista had finally wrenched herself free of Gus and Bootsie, her head was spinning with their ceaseless chatter. Had they both taken amphetamines or what? Gus had made another call to discuss his tennis-coaching schedule. There certainly had been no opportunity to open up any sort of discussion with Bootsie about her past. A soft drizzle had begun to fall. As Calista walked up Charles Street, she wondered how she had ever been so presumptuous as to think she could have gone in and begun talking about all this stuff with Bootsie.

The wet brick smell rose from the sidewalk. The rain came down harder. It felt good. She was not wearing a jacket and soon her blouse stuck to her skin. She felt cool at last. Ringlets of wet hair plastered her forehead and there were rivulets running down to her eyebrows. She turned up Mt. Vernon Street. The trees dripped and the windowpanes in the tall brick houses were slick. If you squinted just so, the inky green of the trees, the dark cobbles of the street, and the brick smeared into a slide of rain-dark colors. It was a very sensual, timeless world. Perhaps she could slip through a loophole into another history, another universe. If there were multiple universes, there could be multiple and simultaneous histories. If only time were not linear but curled back on itself in loops so that there was no such thing as "progress" or "advancement" in a chronological sense, then there would be this place where time stood still, at the center of things, where you could meet another aspect of yourself in this motionless place with complete understanding. Just supposing, thought Calista, I have a nineteenth-century counterpart who lived on this hill. She turned into Louisburg Square and continued her thought: Instead of being products of time, we would be nuances of, say, light or passion; then time and chronologies might be irrelevant.

Just ahead, Calista spotted a cluster of dark umbrellas at the end of the walk of number 18, the Kingsleys'. A dark car was pulled up. Calista approached.

There was the meanest lady in Boston, her mouth a trembling red slash. A nurse held an umbrella over her to shield her from the rain. "What do you mean we can't get in? We don't have the right set of keys? I thought you squared this with Gus, Harley, you fool! Bambi, call Gus now."

"I tried, Grummy. There was no answer." Bambi looked away from Cornelia Parkington and spotted Calista approaching. "Oh hi! We can't reach Gus—although I know this isn't his day for coaching at St. Bennett's. You don't by any chance have a key to the Kingsleys'?"

"Who's that?" growled Cornelia.

"Calista Jacobs, Grummy. You know, the one who is the Baldwins' friend and is staying there this summer."

"The Jewish one?"

Holy smoke! thought Calista. Had she actually heard that correctly? The shrewish one perhaps? Bambi colored and Harley stopped his intense perusal of the set of keys he was holding. He coughed loudly. "I think we should be going."

"I think we should not," barked Cornelia. "I want to check on that painting. If they stole those Japanese things out of here, it is not secure. If anything happens to the portrait, I'm going to hold you responsible. Figure out a way to get in, Harley."

"I can't break in, Cornelia."

"Call Bootsie," Cornelia snapped. "She might have a key."

Harley groaned. "Let me run down to Charles Street. There must be a pay phone down there."

"Oh, don't do that," Calista said. "Come on into the Baldwins'. You can use the phone."

"How kind of you," Harley said.

"Uh . . . would the rest of you like to come in out of the rain?"

"Oh no, that won't be necessary," Bambi replied quickly, rolling her eyes in a manner that indicated good old Grummy could drown out here, for all she cared.

Harley followed Calista in to number 16. "There's a phone right in there, in the study."

"Oh thank you. This is very kind of you . . . and er . . . uh . . ." Calista knew what was coming. "Don't mind Mrs. Parkington she's just a . . ."

"An ignorant bitch." Calista finished the sentence. She would not tolerate excuses in such matters.

"I wasn't going to put it quite that way . . . but—"

"Well, I did. So you don't have to now."

Harley blinked at her through his horned-rimmed glasses as perhaps if he was seeing something for the very first time. He then turned and went into the study to use the phone. "Busy," he said. "Do you mind if I try again?"

"No, not at all. Be my guest," Calista called in. She was sorting through the mail.

"Uh . . . is this your work here on this board?"

Calista walked in. She had set up a drafting table by the window. On it was a half-finished painting of the artificial bird that had been made to replace the nightingale in the story. Calista had painted it sitting on a silk cushion set beside the emperor's throne.

"Yeah."

"You do this for a living? Oh, by the way, I'm Harley Bishop, attorney for the Kingsleys."

"I'm Calista Jacobs, and yes, I do this for a living."

"Why of course. I have heard of you. I believe my children,

when they were younger, read your books. Why, you're famous!" His face seemed to brighten and he looked at her again. "What is this picture for?"

"*The Emperor and the Nightingale.* It's a spread where they've just brought the mechanical one to the emperor."

"Gee, I'm not sure whether I'm familiar with that story."

"Oh it's an old Andersen tale, basically about power and obsession with perfection and art and artifice—perhaps a tad like Cornelia out there."

This reference seemed to bring old Harley back to reality. "Oh, I'll try Boots again. God, I hope she has a key."

He dialed the number. "Ah, Boots! Harley Bishop, dear. I'll tell you why I'm calling. Dear Aunt Cornelia . . . yes, you guessed it . . . having fits about the Mather portrait. She just wants to check on it. We can't get in. My keys don't seem to work. By chance, do you have one? Splendid . . . what? Oh, there is one here? Yes . . . yes. Well, as a matter of fact, I'm standing with Ms. Jacobs right now. Calling from Will Baldwin's study. Terrific."

There was a key hidden behind the greenhouse in the back by the hedge. Calista took Harley out through the Baldwins' back door to the Connecting Gardens. He was back in less than a minute, just as Charley Jacobs came walking through the front door.

"Oh hi, Charley. Meet Harley Bishop. He's a lawyer for the Kingsleys."

Charley nearly gulped, but he recovered fairly quickly. Was this weird or what? He hadn't even hacked in yet and here was this guy. He even had a fragment of a copy of Harley's phone log upstairs, culled from the Dumpster in the alley behind Post Office Square. Rudy Kingsley was supposed to have the disc this afternoon. God, he couldn't have blown it yet. He trusted there was some other agenda going on here.

"You're drenched, Charley. Maybe you'd better go upstairs and dry off."

"Yeah, and I have to meet . . . uh . . . Matthew . . . soon. They let us off early because of the rain."

"Will you be home for dinner?"

"Uh . . . no."

"Nice meeting you, Charley." Harley said as Charley turned to go upstairs.

"Oh, nice meeting you, Mr. Bishop." This was absolutely too weird. Wait until Rudy heard this.

"Well, I better go. I can't thank you enough, Calista." He shook her hand. His grip lingered. This guy's going to call, Calista thought. Damn it. She always could tell when they were going to call. He was attractive in that tight-ass WASP Elliot Richardson way. Not the way that appealed to Calista. Shoot! She wished Archie would come back. This was one complication she simply did not need. And no denying it: She was horny as all get out.

# 25

"You don't say, Leon . . . no . . . my this is a coincidence . . . but totally unanticipated. So you say that it was a woman's voice and she insists on anonymity? And you are sure that she most likely did not have the second netsuke at the time of her initial call? Interesting . . . Oh! My young friend has just arrived. Yes, I'll be talking to you, and you keep me posted if you get any other phone calls from Madame X."

Charley had been shown to a smaller room off the library at the Harvard Club on Commonwealth Avenue, where he found Rudy.

"Welcome to my Boston office. Quite convenient. We have everything here one needs to carry on business—phone, fax, copy machine down the hall."

"You got the disc back to them?"

"Yes, I messengered it to Harley first thing this morning."

"I just met Harley."

"You what?" Rudy's pale eyes widened in surprise.

"Get this: He was at the Baldwins' house, using the phone. Mom let him use it because he had come with some old biddy to check on some picture in the Kingsleys' house and his key didn't work."

"Cornelia had him over there." Rudy's face darkened. "At two hundred and fifty an hour, Cornelia is hauling Harley over to number Eighteen to check up on that ridiculous painting." Rudy pulled a saffron-colored silk handkerchief that appeared to be the size of a small towel from his pocket. He sank onto a settee, rolled his head back, and began to mop his brow.

"Are you all right?" Charley asked. Just his luck for this gay geezer to have a heart attack on him.

"I'm fine. Believe me, if there is such a thing as reincarnation, I think I would honestly prefer to come back as Tammy Faye Bakker than as a member of this family. Every day is a trial; every day one must use one's wit and grit just to survive the sheer outrageousness of this family and their peculiarities, their neuroses. It eats you alive if you don't. So what do you wind up with—the survivors—people like me and Cornelia. But I swear if that bitch wasn't wheelchair-bound, I wouldn't put murder past her."

"You wouldn't?" Charley asked.

"Throughout her life, this woman has committed a thousand and one little murders, little bloodless murders."

"What do you mean?"

"Oh, my dear boy, it's too complicated to go into."

"But she's from the other side of the family, isn't she? She's not directly related to you?"

"Not exactly. But as with all these Boston families, the genealogies get intertwined at certain points. That is really the source of the problem over the Cotton Mather portrait. Both families, the Parkingtons and the Kingsleys, can trace a lineal descent to that loathsome man. You know, he was best known for his zeal for hunting down witches and his experiments in curing the afflicted girls—pseudoscience being the last refuge of pinched minds. The problem was, the best witch was yet to come."

"Cornelia?" Charley said.

"Yes, and Bambi, her granddaughter, would be a close second. Anyhow, enough of that. Weren't you supposed to bring your computer?"

"I did," Charley said, taking off his backpack.

"In that? It fits in there?"

"It's not a mainframe, just a laptop. Have you called Harley and had him load the disc up to show the changes?"

"Yes. Actually, it was his secretary, Mildred."

"It doesn't matter who it was just as long as we got it into the system."

"Well, yes. I did it rather smoothly. I just called up and told them that the accession number on the small gold minotaur must be followed by a letter indicating a new system we were trying out with Greek antiquities of a certain size. I also corrected a small detail concerning a tax benefit over a gift to the Tate. All quite convincing, I thought."

"Social engineering," Charley said.

"What?"

"Social engineering. I knew you'd be great at it."

"What is it?"

"What you just did with Mildred. It is a hacker's best tool. You pose as someone else or you make up a phony question that gives you a foot in the door."

"But really, Charley, *you* did that, or at least you're going to get us in."

"No. I created the door, a back door. You got your foot in it through your social-engineering skills with Mildred. I couldn't have done that. It's not my thing. I've got friends who can. You talk real smooth and your accent and all. It helps. There's this woman, Barbara, she's really famous. She was actually a prostitute, but she was queen of the phone phreaks. She got right into the heart of the Pacific Bell system. She downloaded a whole set of missile-firing parameters and maintenance schedules for intercontinental missiles. She knew exactly how the Pentagon was connected with the Bell system. She worked with a gang out of L.A., but she was the perfect social engineer. Well, seeing as she was a prostitute, maybe it came with the territory." Charley had a bemused look on his face. Rudy nearly burst out laughing. He had never seen anything quite so quixotically charming as this boy.

"Okay now, are you going to show me how it works?"

"Sure enough. Let me plug in."

It took Charley less than a minute to plug in his laptop and modem, then boot up. He dialed the number for Hopkins, Bishop and Creeth.

"What's that?" Rudy said excitedly. He had pulled up a chair next to the table where Charley was working. He leaned forward and recrossed his legs. The gray screen had brightened.

**WELCOME TO HOPKINS, BISHOP AND CREETH. WARNING: THIS SYSTEM IS FOR THE EXCLUSIVE USE OF HBC FIRM EMPLOYEES ONLY. ANY ABUSE WILL BE PROSECUTED UNDER THE COMPUTER IN- TRUSION ACT 1039.**

"That's supposed to scare us," Charley said.

"But it doesn't?" Rudy replied, his voice swelling with excitement. He wiggled in his chair and recrossed his legs again.

"Right. We're tough dudes here."

"Oh, this is so exciting, Charley, I can hardly stand it."

Charley was excited, too. There was nothing quite like the high of busting into a bureaucracy. Their sheer smugness was adrenaline into the veins of any technocowboy riding through cyber space. Give those kids with the funny haircuts and the plastic pen holders white hats, spurs, and chaps and they would carry on the best of the American frontier tradition. Only now it was an electronic frontier. Nonetheless, these kids were absolutely soaked with a heroism as old as the country, a heroism associated with cowboys, mountain men, and original thinkers who had stood up against rigid no-balls institutions; it could be the Bell system, the Pentagon, Wall Street, NASA, big industrial complexes, or fat-cat law firms—mainframe guys. But all of the guys in these places set themselves up as an "information priest-hood"; they treated knowledge and information as an elitist com-modity—just like their fucking elitist clubs, one of which Char-ley now sat in, and the university in which his late father had held the Cowles Chair of Particle Physics.

**USER NAME:**

"What's Mildred's last name again?"

"Hennessey."

Charley typed in her name.

**PASSWORD:**

**BIJOU**

"That's French." Charley looked up.

"I know," Rudy replied. "Is it going to work?"

"Of course. Eighteen months ago, I could have set up a pro-gram to generate passwords randomly to get Mildred's word. But a lot of places now have programs that can detect when that is being done. These folks probably don't. They seem old-style. They don't monitor this thing at all. I can tell. But better safe than sorry. This is the cleanest way possible."

"I still don't understand what you did exactly."

"It was easy. On that disc you gave me, I created a backdoor into the system. I wrote a little virus in a computer language—*C plus, plus.*"

"But a virus? That makes me nervous."

"Don't worry. It's not destructive and it's containable. I'll de-lete the whole thing when we're through. No trace. Besides, even if it got loose, it wouldn't hurt anything. Not terminal. I just made it so that this password of mine, *Bijou,* is recognizable along with whatever Mildred's other word is. Think of it like a Trojan horse—that's what they sometimes call them—to get us into the city. Okay. Get ready. Here we go. What do you want to see?"

"Call up Elliot Kingsley's will."

Charley raked through the files. There were nearly one hundred documents under Kingsley. He found the file Rudy had asked for.

Rudy got out his reading glasses. "Yes, just as I remembered. Quite standard. It passes to the widow first. And now that will pass on to the kids through Quintana. They should have put part of that in an irrevocable trust. I told Kingie that before he died. Taxwise, it would have been beneficial, and, of course, it precludes squabbling. Okay, dear boy, let's go to Quintana."

"Oh man . . . there's a lot here," Charley said, looking at the files listed. "Lot of action in the last year."

"Lot of action in the last two months," Rudy said. "This could be interesting."

It took hours, and for Charley, it was not that interesting. He felt like a digital drudge, but Rudy was fascinated. "That bitch! Wouldn't you know that Queenie would be that kind. Changing her will just slightly every three weeks and probably calling everybody in for little family dinners to announce the favored heir of the month. But she certainly seems to have favored Gus consistently. She always was soft on him. Poor Boots. Let's call up Boots's file and get a peek at some of her assets."

Charley found a file for Bootsie.

"Well, isn't that sweet," Rudy said sarcastically. "Queenie gave the main house of Nohqwha to Bootsie."

"That's not good?" Charley asked.

"Not for Bootsie, I don't think. It is not a repository of happy memories—to say the least. It was where her sister Muffy hung herself, for one thing. And how would Bootsie ever maintain it? Her portfolio, at least what I see of it here, looks rather pathetic. Her major asset is the Brookline house. She apparently has a second mortgage out on that. See, I told Kingie that if he had set up an irrevocable trust, real estate like that could have gone into it and it would have relieved Bootsie of a terrible burden. What else does she have to show here? Good God, railroad stocks! How they treat the women in this family! Look, her best stuff is what I gave her years ago—a rental property in the South End, Charming Shoppes—those clothes for chubby ladies are still doing well. Good grief—she's still got the Wang. I told her to get rid of that."

At 10:30, Malcolm, the steward, arrived with a tray—Lapsang souchong tea and a plate of smoked salmon for Rudy; Coke and home fries for Charley.

"Gee, these are fat," Charley said, picking up one of the fries. "Not like McDonald's." He took a bite of one of the fries. "Did you ever hear about Fry Guy?"

"Fry Guy?" Rudy repeated.

"Yeah. He's this incredible kid from Indiana. He's in federal prison now. I mean, I don't want you to think I would actually ever do anything like this, but the guy really has style."

"Yes?" Rudy said. "I'm waiting." He slid his thumb under his suspenders.

"Well, this kid, he's in the Legion of Doom."

"Legion of Doom? Is this going to be an S and M story?"

"S and M?"

"Sadomasochism."

"Oh no no noooo, nothing like that. This was all good clean fun till he got busted. Well, there's the phone-sex part."

"Phone sex?"

"Yeah, Tina in Queens—but I'm jumping ahead."

"Well, by all means, don't do that. Let's savor the story." Rudy leaned forward and stabbed a slice of smoked salmon. He arranged it on a piece of dark rye and then took a tiny spoon and spread some mustard sauce on it. It was all so dainty and neat, Charley felt kind of gross by comparison. He had just dribbled some catsup on his shirt from the fat fry.

"Well, anyhow, the Legion of Doom is just this underground bulletin board. You know, a pirate board. I explained to you about these electronic bulletin boards. Pirate ones, you know, do stuff that is either slightly illegal—copies of games or manuals, stolen passwords, how to get into systems—or all the way illegal, like getting credit card numbers. Some of the boards are really heavy, anarchistic boards.

"*Phrack,* a phreak hacking magazine, shows up on a lot of these boards. It is considered by the feds a major bad-attitude outfit, along with the Legion of Doom. In any case, Fry Guy was a typical Legion of Doom dude. He lived out in Indiana. He was just about sixteen years old, and he is considered like majorly wicked now by the feds."

"What did he do?"

"Many things. He got his name from one particular stunt when he lifted a password or something and logged in through a local McDonald's to their mainframe. He did some social engineering, came in as a manager, and gave two of his friends nice raises."

"And he got caught?"

"Well, finally, but not for that. He actually got caught for receiving stolen goods through electronic credit-card fraud. He was an expert at raiding information from credit card–reporting agencies. He really broke track in a whole new kind of wire fraud."

"His mother must have been so proud," Rudy said dryly.

"He knew all the tricks of switching stations. He combined his credit card know-how with his switch tricks, and man, the guy could have had Wall Street by the balls. But see, like a lot of phreaks and crackers, they just can't shut up; they have to brag. He was so full of himself. But with each job, it was like he was driven to top his last performance."

"I'm waiting for the phone sex," Rudy said primly, and took a sip of his tea.

"Here it is: Southern Bell is notoriously slipshod in their security. There was a probation office down in Florida somewhere and it seemed as if every call that was for that office somehow got switched to a phone-sex worker named Tina up in New York."

"Good God! How did that happen?"

"Fry Guy. It was really before he got into the heavy stuff of stealing money through wires. He was just having some fun. But you know, it would be bad if someone was having a heart attack and you called nine-one-one and all of a sudden you got switched to Tina. Fry Guy got into the central switching station for Bell

South and reprogrammed the works. They got kind of paranoid when they found out what he had done to their 'state-of-the-art' digital switching station. Actually, Legion of Doom guys had been traipsing around in Bell South switches for months before that. It was Fry Guy who just pulled off the ultimate stunt."

"Where do you draw the line on this sort of thing?"

"You mean me personally?"

"Yes, you, Charley Jacobs."

"I told you, I don't trash as in crash and I don't steal. But I don't buy this shit of theirs that there's like, you know, a priesthood that can control knowledge and information completely. I'm thinking it out, have been thinking it out for a long time. What is the meaning of the words *intellectual property?* I hate the notion of forbidden knowledge. I know that nothing I have ever done electronically has hurt anyone, deprived them of anything—information, money—anything."

"So you do have this rather rough-hewn ethos, rules."

"Yeah, ethos. Rules, I'm not sure. Rules are for rodents, as they say. But yeah, I got standards—moral standards. The best hackers do. You never hear about the best hackers. They're very adult. They don't brag. They've got beautiful skills. They don't go in for fancy hardware. They get these banged-up junkers and they make them hum like Porsches. It's like my dad's friend Freeman Dyson, this physicist at Princeton. He had this totally cool idea about going into space—this was years ago, before anyone had ever done it. He was a lot older than my dad, but Dad had had him as a professor when he was at the Institute, and he said that Dyson hated all the money that NASA was spending. Dyson's idea of a great spacecraft was something that people put together in their backyards—you know, bits and pieces of old junk, scrap hardware. One of his designs had the thing powered with atomic bombs—can you believe it? It was before people were environmentally aware, needless to say. But my dad and I used to make rockets like that, not atomic ones, just things pieced together with cardboard tubes, the kind that come inside toilet-paper rolls, and chicken wire and we messed around with crystal radios a lot. That's really the way it is with the best hackers: They slap their machines together with gaffers' tape, old chips, fishing line. I got some of my mom's fishing line in this thing. You wind up with something fabulous. 'Digital dragsters,' they call them."

"But what about the rules? Why are rules for rodents?" Rudy asked.

"Well, rules are more concrete. They deal with real things. See, you got to understand where we are now isn't quite real." Charley gestured at the computer screen. It showed a letter concerning changes in Quintana Kingsley's will.

"What do you mean not real?"

"It's cyber space. Cyber space isn't real."

"Are you saying it's a state of mind?"

"Sort of. But it's not real like a glove or a hat is real, or even money is real. You can't hold it in your hand. Cyber space is electrical space. And it is a place where things do happen that affect people and the world. It used to be like this dark narrow tunnel with two-way traffic. It was the space between two telephones. You could talk, one person to the other, transmit and receive. But now, in the past thirty years—well, twenty years—it kind of crossbred or maybe interbred with computers. It's like a whole new species has evolved. The space is no longer this narrow little tunnel. It's like this weird bright place with these electronic tentacles stretching out everywhere. Cyber space is to the electronic landscape what the rain forest is to earth—a virtual powerhouse; the rainforest for bio diversity—oxygen and all that; cyber space for information. Both are primal generating systems."

"Very interesting," Rudy said. "Well, we better get back to what we're looking for."

"You want me to download these files here—the changes in the will—to my computer?"

"Yes. I suppose that might be helpful. Evidence, I guess." Rudy's voice dropped. There was a slight melancholy tinge to it that Charley could not miss.

"What's wrong?"

"It just seems that there is a pattern here of favoring Gus over Bootsie. Bootsie looks virtually, or comparatively, penniless. And it's difficult for me to explain to you, but Bootsie has very substantial reason to be profoundly angry with her family."

"So you think this gives her a reason to kill her mother?"

"Possibly. But certainly to steal those netsukes. If she were cut out of the will and is indeed in such bad financial straits as she appears to be here ... well, the netsukes, I am told, could get her close to one million dollars."

Charley whistled low. "Not looking good for Bootsie."

"No, it isn't. But there is one thing that troubles me."

"What's that?"

"I can't quite put my finger on it at the moment, but it has something to do with the actual theft. It is possible that the pair of netsukes were taken at two different times. That doesn't quite make sense."

Charley shifted nervously in his seat. He thought of his mom and her visit to the greenhouse when she had seen the woman intruder. Maybe he should tell Rudy.

"Look at this," Rudy said. "On July twenty-seventh, little more than week before Quintana was murdered, she changed her will to favor Gus substantially. Talk about the lion's share. He stood to inherit three million in cash assets and stocks—and that is not counting the house on Louisburg Square, which could easily fetch close to another million. Not fair. It would make me mad."

"But maybe it made Gus impatient. Maybe he wanted his hands on that money. This could be a motive for him, too, you know," Charley said.

"Yes, that's true. But Gus wasn't desperate. He had already been favored. See, being older than Bootsie, he had already come into a trust at fifty."

"Will she get one when she turns fifty?"

There was a knock on the door. It was Malcolm. "Mr. Kingsley, could you step out here a moment?"

"Why of course, Malcolm." Rudy turned to Charley. "I'll be right back."

When Rudy Kingsley walked into the room five minutes later, he looked ten years older. Pale and shaking, he sat down. He put his hand lightly on Charley's arm. "You were asking will Bootsie come into a trust when she is fifty—unfortunately she will never be fifty. That was the police. She hung herself tonight. Jamie discovered her. There was apparently a note confessing to the murder of Quintana."

"Jamie found her?"

"Yes. I have to get right over there for the poor kid. Perhaps we should tell your mother. There are very few stable women in this family. I think that your mother might prove helpful at this point."

"Yeah," Charley said softly. He had this inexorable urge to cry. This wasn't cyber space. This was real—so real. This was just like a few years ago when the unbelievable news about his own father came. This was horrible. He wanted his mom.

# 26

Charley had insisted on coming with her, and Calista didn't like
the idea one bit. On the other hand, leaving him by himself was
not at all appealing. He had seemed to shrink before her eyes; he
was as pale and wispy as a little kid, his eyes full of fear. It had
brought back too much and he needed to be near her. And
Calista needed to be near him. They were strong together. The
thought struck her as odd. But it came in response to this last
horror. She wondered whether the Kingsleys had ever been
strong together. They seemed thoroughly blown apart; ato-
mized—this was their natural condition. And in that condition,
they thrived on one another's weaknesses and vulnerabilities.
Deceit and distrust were at the core of family dynamics, the twin
handmaids of their peculiar family neurosis. *Neurosis* was too
nice a word. They were sick all right, but they had let it go on—
eating up the family, innocent victims like Bootsie. She supposed
Bootsie wasn't so innocent. Apparently, there had been a note
confessing to her mother's murder.

* * *

When they arrived at Lockwood Street, an ambulance was just pulling away. Good, Calista thought. At least there won't be a body around. Malcolm was driving them. Rudy and Charley had swung by Louisburg Square to pick her up and then they had continued to Brookline. There were three police cars pulled up and a BPD van. Lights were flashing and a uniformed police officer met them coming up the walk.

"I'm Jamie's great-uncle, Rudy Kingsley, and these are close friends. How is Jamie?"

"There's a doctor with him now. You folks can go right in. He's in the living room still."

"Still?" asked Calista.

"That's where he found his mother. She hung herself from a lighting fixture."

Calista gasped as they entered the living room. Although the body had been removed, her shock was as profound as if it was still there, swinging from the noose that hung from the thick brass arm of the chandelier. A kitchen stool was directly underneath the chandelier. The noose seemed strangely obscene, derisive of the fine taste and style of the room. Calista realized with a jolt that bordered on anger that Bootsie had hung herself directly across from the beautiful Japanese scrolls. She half-expected those cranes to metamorphose into nightmarish gargoyles and come screeching out from their tranquil flight, leaving the waterfall behind to churn with blood. The room had changed in a distinct yet unnameable way. Everything had disintegrated into disorder, confusion, chaos. Or was there an unknown order here, a pattern? Had Bootsie's life been ordered toward this end—no matter what? She remembered Bootsie sitting in the ivory brocade-covered wing chair, her head tilted back against the braided piping that edged its contours. She looked at the scroll again. The cranes flew on and the waterfall cascaded in another world, one far away, of order and purpose. That world was still intact. Calista did not know which was more real. And then she saw Jamie sitting rigid on the sofa where she herself had sat a day before.

Rudy had gone over to him and had put an arm around his shoulders. But Jamie stared ahead, his eyes unblinking, his head bent forward toward that noose as if trying to comprehend the lopsided oval, the space of nothingness that had ended his mother's life.

There were people walking about in circular patterns vaguely familiar to Calista: a photographer, a woman with a clipboard, another one with a tape measure. There was the crackle of voices coming over transmitters and cellular phones. Charley sat down on the sofa on the other side of Jamie. Calista moved with him. She was not aware of walking. It was rather as if she were a magnetic filing in Charley's wake. She felt herself crouching in front of Jamie. She was very aware of Rudy's scent—toasted almonds. It was a cologne that he wore. And she saw his thin, wrinkled hand with its age spots stroking Jamie's forearm. She heard herself telling Jamie that he should come back and stay with them for as long as he wanted, until his father came or whatever.

It was all like a dream and it felt no more real than if she had been a figure in one of the ink-wash scrolls. She heard a police officer ask to talk to Rudy. It was very odd. She could hear more than one conversation. It was as if a sudden clarity had washed through the room or through her brain. They were talking now about time of death, 5:00 P.M.; she heard the words *open and shut*. She presumed that these modified the word *suicide*. It was as if the sentences in which they were speaking were being parsed as she listened. Modifiers floated out with clarity: direct objects, adjectives, adverbs—*instant, instantly*. They had used both words. She listened carefully. That would be important. It would be nice if they could tell poor Jamie that his mother had died instantly, that it was over within a fraction of a second. Then a silent harsh laugh crashed through her brain. Yes, how nice, a derisive voice muttered. After years of pain to have it all end quickly—is that the reward? A swift and sudden death by your own hand? There was a note, yes. Detective Froines had the note.

# 27

"What do you mean he can't be reached? Everybody is someplace; therefore, everybody can be reached. This is the last decade of the twentieth century. Making contact with an extraterrestrial is just around the corner."

"Jamie's dad is on a safari with his family and he is in the one region at this time where he is totally inaccessible."

Rudy closed his eyes and pursed his lips as if to damper down his own dismay.

"I have a feeling this whole fucking family has been inaccessible to its children for aeons. Shit, this is absolutely preposterous," Calista fumed.

"I know, Calista. I know too well."

Titty, who had remained quiet, sighed heavily. "The poor child." She nearly moaned. "I thought it was bad being a girl in this family, but I guess in the final analysis, no one is really safe."

Calista looked up at Titty. She knew on one level what she

meant, but on another, there was something very unsettling about it. Titty was right. It had been the girls who had been the victims, or so it was believed, until now. But why had she found what Titty had just said so disturbing? There was something prodding at the back of her mind. She knew she was not thinking this whole thing through the way she ought to be.

"Has he eaten anything?" Rudy inquired.

"What? What did you say?" Calista asked. She had not been listening. The notion of females as victims was disturbing her in a new way, as if there was some new wrinkle in it.

"I said, Has Jamie eaten anything yet?"

"Oh yes, we have made some headway on that front."

"He still won't see a doctor, I take it?" Rudy asked.

"No. He actually won't see anybody except us. Gus came over. So did Bambi. One of his teachers from Poulton called, but Jamie wouldn't talk to him. It puts Charley and me in sort of an odd position. I mean, why will he not see or talk to any of them but here he is with us? Not that I mind it."

"Maybe he's finally around some sensible people, a family that knows how to be a family. Did that ever occur to you?"

"Well, maybe. He even walked over with Charley to the swan boats this morning."

"Has he cried at all?" Titty asked.

"No."

"That's the most worrisome thing of all, I'd say," Rudy replied.

"You've talked to the police?" Calista asked suddenly.

"Yes." Rudy took out a handkerchief and wiped his brow. "I read the note. She made it quite clear that she had killed Quintana, and said she could not go on living."

"She didn't say why she killed her?" Calista asked.

"I guess she didn't feel it really required an explanation. It was a remarkably terse note. There was nothing about Jamie in it at all."

"I think that's weird," Calista said. "And I think it's even weirder that she would kill herself where she did, where Jamie could find her so easily. She might have been alcoholic and mentally damaged, but I just can't believe she would do this terrible thing with such total disregard for Jamie."

"Yes, but no telling what state she was in," Titty said.

"I do wonder," Calista said softly.

"Wonder what?" Rudy asked.

"What state she was in?"

Jamie just needed some clear space, time to think things out. He had lost count of how many times they had been around the duck pond. Jamie sat in the very back of the boat, just in front of Charley, or if it was a full load, he stood next to Charley while he pedaled. Art, the supervisor, didn't seem to mind. He would tell Art that he would take care of bedding down the swans that night. He actually enjoyed that part of the day the best. You swept out the floor between the benches, made sure there were no weeds on the paddle blades, then wiped down the swans, their heads, the lovely curve of their necks, the wings. Now, however, he just stared ahead and listened to the sound of the water churning through the paddle wheels as Charley pedaled. Had his mom really thought that he had killed Grandma? Is that why she wrote that note and then killed herself, to protect him? He had to sort this thing out. It was so confusing. He was getting things all mixed up. He had found that letter when he had taken out the trash before he had gone to work that morning, the morning of the day his mom had killed herself. It was a rough draft, printed out from his printer but not complete. What had surprised him was the "Dear Gus." His mother would never call Gus dear, even if it was the standard way to begin a letter. She hated her brother. And although hardly loving, hatred was certainly not the tone of this letter. Desperate—that was the tone. He had the letter tucked away in his pocket now. He did not need to take it out to remember the words.

Dear Gus,
I am willing to put the past behind. You are right—

the damage is done and nothing in terms of legal re-
dress can repair what you have done to Jamie. I
thought the worst had happened, but this is worse. I
cannot believe that the police have any kind of evidence that could link him to Mummy's death. I still
can't quite follow what you are saying that led you to
believe this, but promise me you will let me know
anything else you hear. I guess you're right about it
being too early to bring in Harley. I don't know where
to turn. I guess, for better or for worse, we're stuck
with each other. It's like a bad joke. Our entire lives
have been a bad joke, Gus. Maybe you have been as
much of a victim as Muffy and I were. You're sick. So
am I, but please help me save Jamie. He is all that I
have to live for. . . .

*Live for, but then she died.* That was the part that Jamie just
could not figure out. And was he supposed to die now? Or was he
supposed to kill? Where had this stuff come from about him killing Grandma? He stared straight ahead. They were approaching
the island where the ducks lived. The little babies, mere fluff
balls earlier in the summer, had fledged their wings. They
weren't swimming as close to their mothers. They were paddling
out in larger circles, until she would come and shoo them back.
Those ducks were saner, better off than he was; there were parts
of nature so uncomplicated and so straightforward as to be almost
brave in their simplicity. That truth overwhelmed him.

Suddenly, Jamie realized that he was through with being sul-
len, angry, damaged. He hated those words. He wanted to be
brave. Within seconds, it became very clear to him: The past had
been bad, but it had been bad largely because he was not in control; the future was going to be worse, if that was possible, but it
was and he knew it—worse things were about to happen to him.
He was being set up for something terrible, just as his mother
had been. She had not killed herself to protect him. She had, if
anything, died in vain, and he was still unprotected. He was

going to have to kill or get killed. He had had it with the other way; he had had it with stupid anger and blaming. It didn't matter anymore. He had to be brave. It was very simple if he looked at it that way. He just had to keep his focus and keep it simple. He had to forget right now, once and for all, the years of humiliation, the horrible things that Gus had done to him.

# 28

She had been sound asleep; she had not been dreaming, at least she didn't recall dreaming. But when she opened her eyes, she could see that noose so clearly—the twists of it. Calista got out of bed and walked to a window. There were curtain cords. She took them and began to twist them. Her left hand was the steadying hand. She made the twists with her right hand counterclockwise. Was this common? It seemed the natural way to do it if you were right-handed. She tried to twist it the other way, clockwise. It didn't feel right. She tried to reverse her hands and use her right hand as the steadying hand and use the left to twist the rope. That was almost impossible. She spent the next twenty minutes trying various knots with the curtain cords. Calista knew a lot of knots and a lot about knot tying, for she tied her own flies for fly-fishing. Those were often very specialized knots. But take the most basic kinds of knots used for tippets, such as a barrel or a surgeon's knot, and take the most elemental part of, say, a barrel knot, where you must wind one end around the standing part. If you were right-handed, you did it one way; if left-handed, you did it another. The string either wound clockwise or counterclockwise. She realized, of course, that in terms of statistical value, her control group was rather small. She would try it tomorrow with Charley, not Jamie. She stared at the knot she had just tied. A new realization began to creep into her mind as she pictured the noose hanging from the chandelier: What did it really matter whether the twists were clockwise or counterclockwise? The knot itself was meticulously, perfectly made. For a woman who was usually well into a quart of vodka by midday, this seemed to constitute a fair bit of manual dexterity.

The phone rang a little after seven. A scratchy voice on the other end cawed, "I understand you're keeping him."

"Who? . . . Who is this?"

"Cornelia Parkington, Diggory Parkington's sister-in-law and Bootsie's aunt. I want to know why Jamie's staying with you. It's not appropriate."

To say this conversation was going poorly was an understatement. What's more, there seemed to be very little hope of getting it back on any "appropriate" track. Calista felt the anger swelling in her. "I would say that there have been a lot of inappropriate things going on in this family for a long time, particularly in recent weeks. I would suggest that you talk to your lawyer, Harley Bishop, concerning Jamie's staying here. But if you want to know why he is . . ."

"Yes I do," Cornelia snapped.

"It's because he wants to." She was about to say good-bye and hang up, but Cornelia barked again.

"And there is the matter of the Cotton Mather portrait."

"What?" Calista was stymied. What in the world could that have to do with Jamie?

"He cannot touch that portrait. It comes down through my branch of the family."

"Fuck Cotton Mather!" Calista slammed down the phone.

Ten minutes later, Harley Bishop called up. "I'm sure we can work this out, Calista."

"As far as I'm concerned, there is nothing to work out. I am not keeping Jamie here. He elected to stay here. It would seem most appropriate to speak with him, but I think he's still asleep. Should I have him call you when he gets up?"

"Yes, yes, do that, and Gus would like to see him, too. Please tell him that."

"I will."

"And . . ." Harley's voice rose just slightly. Here it comes, Calista thought.

"I know, given the circumstances, this might seem inappropriate." Calista rolled her eyes. What was this obsession with appropriateness? "But would you be interested in meeting me for a drink this evening? I should be finished at the office around seven-fifteen. And I'm really so intrigued by your work as an illustrator." Baloney, Calista thought. "I'd love to talk to you more about it and just thought perhaps a drink at the Ritz . . ."

Calista's instincts were to say no, but this was the Kingsley family lawyer. Charley and Rudy had told Calista about Charley's electronic peregrinations through the Hopkins, Bishop and Creeth computers and what they had found in terms of the recent will changes. She supposed she might be able to gab a little about children's book illustration and then, as Charley would say, do some social engineering and perhaps find out something else. She still simply did not believe that Bootsie had killed Quintana. She was beginning now to doubt Bootsie's suicide.

"Okay, but listen, one thing."

"Certainly."

"Keep that old bat out of my hair."

"You mean Cornelia?"

"Precisely. And more important, keep her out of Jamie's hair. The kid just does not need her right now. He needs his dad, wherever he is."

"We're trying on that front."

"Okay. See you around seven-thirty at the Ritz."

No sooner had she hung up than the phone rang once more. She hesitated picking it up. It might be Cornelia at the other end.

She could picture her talons grasping the receiver. Oh would that the bitch's wheelchair roll into the Charles!

"Hello."

"Rudy here, dear. May I come over right away for breakfast? In the confusion, there is an important piece of information I entirely forgot about. Make sure Jamie is up and functioning as well as can be hoped."

"Yes. Yes, of course."

"You are sure of this?" Calista asked, pouring herself another cup of coffee.

"I am not sure, but Leon Mauritz is fairly sure. However, the important thing is"—Rudy turned to Jamie—"your mother was an expert in this area. She, of all people, would know that those two netsukes were most valuable as a pair. Only a neophyte would steal just one."

"So then why would they steal just one?" Calista asked. "I mean, if they were sitting there together on the shelf, why not take two, even if the one was slightly damaged?"

"The only reason I could think is that the person was trying to set up a motive for the killing of Quintana—robbery. It would appear perhaps that the robbery was interrupted if one was left behind."

"Interrupted?" Charley said. "But she was murdered in the greenhouse and the netsukes were in the living room."

"True." Rudy paused and closed his eyes. He tapped a pencil on a piece of paper. He made a number 1 and underscored it. "But what we do know, or, according to Leon, what we can be ninety-nine percent sure of is that the netsukes were taken at two separate times and"—he then wrote down the numeral 2 under the one—"number two, whoever took the netsukes was not an expert in Asian art. Number three, Leon's caller was a woman."

Calista looked nervously across at Charley. He swallowed. The time had come for her to tell what she had seen in the greenhouse on that night shortly after Quintana's murder.

"Wait a second," she said, "I have to show you something."

She got up and went to the pantry. She opened up an empty tin canister used for sugar. Inside was a small plastic bag and in the bag was the garter.

She held out her hand with the plastic bag containing the garter. "I found this in the greenhouse a few days after Quintana was murdered."

Calista told the story of the woman she had seen walking through as she hid behind the bags of mulch and fertilizer.

"So, in short, you witnessed, or possibly witnessed, the theft of the second netsuke," Rudy said. He then turned to Jamie. "Does the description sound anything like your mother?"

"No, not at all. For one thing, I don't think my mom wore garters. I mean, I think she just wore those pull-on kinds of stockings."

"Panty hose," Calista offered, then added, "and probably not in eighty-five degree summer heat."

"Yeah," said Jamie. "And, like Uncle Rudy said, she was an expert. She would have taken both of them and not just one."

"I guess I should tell the police about this, but I suppose they could get me on withholding evidence."

"Well, we should really ask Harley," Rudy said.

"Oh God, I'm having a drink with him."

"You are?"

"Yes. He called and asked me this morning."

"I presume it has something to do with all this."

"I don't know why you presume that. Why, is he married?"

"The last I heard, he was."

"Oh dear, I should have known."

"Listen, Calista. Hold off telling him right away. I want to figure a few more things out."

"So do I," said Calista. "I've been thinking about that Lieutenant O'Hare—was that his name? One of the detectives the other night?"

"Something Irish," Rudy answered vaguely.

Jamie listened to Calista and Rudy talking. Everyone was trying to help him, trying to help his mother, as much as one can help a dead person, clear her name. They were convinced that his mother had not killed his grandmother. He knew that he should tell them about the letter. But if he showed them the letter, then he would have to tell about Gus and the things Gus had done to him. He wasn't sure he could do that yet. He knew he had to be brave. But this was another kind of bravery.

Calista looked over at Jamie. A little tick had begun to kick around his jaw. His eyes shifted nervously and he picked at the bag with the garter. Something was disturbing him. She didn't know what. But the garter was triggering something.

"Oh, by the way, Jamie, when Harley called this morning, he said that your Uncle Gus wanted to see you."

"Well, I don't want to see him," Jamie barked, then colored deeply.

Everyone left—the boys for the swan boats, Rudy for a special meeting at Harley's office to talk to him about the meager estate that Bootsie had left and how he might supplement what was left for Jamie. Calista began to clear away the dishes, her mind turning over the meaning of everything she had learned so far. She picked up the piece of paper on which Rudy had scribbled his notes concerning the netsuke thefts. There were three points: The thefts had occurred at separate times, the thief was not an expert, and finally, the thief was a woman—a woman who wore garters. There was a fourth point, however! Why hadn't she ever thought of this before? She ran to a calendar hanging on the wall over the sink. Yes! The theft had occurred on a Thursday. She turned back the calendar. Quintana had been murdered on a Thursday, the first Thursday in August. She flipped the calendar forward. And Bootsie McPhee had committed suicide on a Thursday. Somebody had Thursdays off. But there was one person who didn't. She had heard the alibi more than once—clearly, deliberately, articulately. Gus Kingsley was always at St. Bennett's on Thursdays; ergo, he could not have done it. He couldn't be a real suspect. St. Bennett's was in New Hampshire, over two hours from Boston. Gus always spent the night when he coached there. The man doth protest too much—about Thursdays. Could she break his alibi? But then where would that get her? The person she had seen when she was in the greenhouse was a woman. Bambi! Bambi and Gus. Was that stretching it? They had seemed rather close when she had seen them together at the reception after the funeral. And hadn't Bambi, too, known Gus's schedule? When they were all on the sidewalk in the pouring rain trying to get into number 18. They were just cousins. Are cousins that familiar with one another's schedules? Maybe cousins who are lovers are. Then where did that leave Cornelia? Calista's stomach turned at the thought of that crone. And what was the motive? Only Bootsie really had a motive: She had the anger, the anger over the sexual abuse she had suffered; the anger over being virtually cut from the will. What the netsukes were valued at was not insignificant. But could or would Bootsie really hang herself? And then there was the noose itself.

Calista put down a dirty coffee cup in the sink. She went to the telephone.

"Lieutenant O'Hare, please. This is Calista Jacobs. Tell him I have some information about the recent suicide of Barbara McPhee." This, of course, was stretching the truth. But Calista had dealt with the police before. She knew they wouldn't return her call unless she left the distinct impression that she knew something they didn't.

A half an hour later, she walked into the Boston police station on Berkeley Street. She was shown immediately into an office. With Lieutenant O'Hare were two plainclothes detectives—the woman who had been at the house following Bootsie's suicide, and a middle-aged man. They were introduced as Detectives Froines and Graham. They looked at her with expressions that were a blend of expectation and calculated indifference. It was an odd mixture. At the same time, there was the distinct feeling that they were going to be very polite and prepare her for some inevitable disappointment: prick pinholes in her theories and watch with ill-concealed satisfaction as the air went out of the balloons.

"So you have some information, Ms. Jacobs?"

She resisted any fudging. She knew they expected her to have sudden doubts, to begin to back off, to declare that the information was perhaps a bit marred, knicked, less than perfect. Well, to hell with them.

"Do you still have the noose that Barbara McPhee used to hang herself?"

"Yes," the woman, Detective Froines, said. "It's in the crime lab."

"Could you get it?"

"Is there a reason for this?" she asked.

Calista opened her eyes wide and said nothing. This woman had an attitude. Maybe she should introduce her to Piss. Lieutenant O'Hare cleared his throat nervously and punched a few numbers on his phone. He leaned toward the intercom screen. Keeping his eyes on Calista, he spoke into the box. "The Brookline suicide. Send up that noose you got from down there. And the photographs, too."

It was just as Calista remembered. Basically, it was a clinch knot with five turns—same knot she often used to tie tippet onto a fly. And the turns were going clockwise. Calista reached into her handbag. She drew out several lengths of twine that she had found in the Baldwins' utility closet.

"I want you to do something for me." She put on her reading glasses so she could see the twine better. "First of all, are you all right-handed here?"

"Not me," said Detective Froines.

"Okay. Now, do you all know how to make a clinch knot? It's used a lot in fly-fishing. I do a lot of fly-fishing." They were watching her, rapt with attention. She was not the usual witness in any sense of the word. She did not appear too eager or too nervous. She worked calmly and efficiently; there was a thoughtfulness to her that bordered on studious. And she was very attractive despite the fact that she wore no makeup, had a mop of silvery hair, and was dressed as chastely as any female police officer.

"I'll demonstrate this knot. It's easy. You'll all get it on the first try." She smiled primly, but underneath the smile, the half glasses, and the mop of hair was a very sexy den mother. That was what O'Hare decided. "Okay," Calista continued. "You take your twine, one end in each hand. You're going to want to form a loop down at the bottom. If we were fly-fishing, you'd be leading this through the eye of a fly. Yeah, you got it, Lieutenant. So do you, folks." She looked over at the two detectives. "Next, I want you to take the piece that is on top and wrap it around the standing part of the leader, say five times. Okay." She looked around. They had begun to wind. Yes, it was just as she'd thought. "All right. You got your five turns; now just bring that end back and pass it through the loop." Calista held hers up.

"So what are we supposed to do now?" Detective Froines asked. "Hang ourselves?"

"Detective, look at your noose. It's different from ours." Detective Froines slid her eyes first to her partner's, then to O'Hare's, and finally to Calista's. She didn't get it. But O'Hare did.

"Lisa's is like the one used in the suicide. Its turns go the opposite way from ours."

"Exactly. We're right-handed. We hold the twine, the standing part of the loop, with our less dominant hand, the left. We use our right hand for the finer motor work of making the turns. It seems that the tendency a hundred percent of the time, in this small control group and with other people I have tried this on, is to make the turns toward your weaker hand—the left hand in all our cases, except for Detective Froines, who is left-handed."

"So?" Lisa Froines asked.

"So Barbara McPhee is right-handed. That noose"—Calista pointed to the tray from the crime lab—"was made by a left-handed person."

"And you feel this is conclusive evidence that Barbara did not commit suicide?"

"Did you check the alcohol level in her blood?"

O'Hare reached for a file. He opened it and ran his eyes down a top sheet. He whistled. "Point two was the level."

"You think she could have tied that knot even if she was left-handed?"

"Someone else could have made it," Detective Graham offered.

"And she could have conveniently found it and then hung herself?" Calista asked.

"It's possible," Detective Graham said. But there was a slight constriction in his voice that suggested substantial doubt.

"Somebody else did make the noose. That is becoming fairly clear," O'Hare said. "As to whether they hung her or she hung herself . . . well, that's another question."

"But the bruises on her neck are completely consistent with those of hanging and not murder," Detective Froines said.

"What are you talking about?" Calista asked.

O'Hare got up and walked from behind his desk to the table where another tray from the crime lab sat. He picked up a manila envelope and took out eight-by-ten glossy prints. He walked over to Calista. The top one showed a curve of white, with a dark inverted V. This was not an abstract design, not a Mark Rothko painting, not calligraphy. The pieces came together slowly for Calista. This was a neck, a human neck through which life had been shut off, extinguished, broken, asphyxiated. It was Barbara McPhee's neck. But Barbara McPhee, the one whose parents had welcomed to the world forty-five years ago and preciously nicknamed Bootsie, no longer existed; the one whose father had raped her and whose mother had let it happen no longer was. Or rather, she was a collection of bruised, decomposing tissues and bones, leaking chemicals on a glinting metal tray in a refrigerated room. No more cute names. The neck and the body it belonged to, the person it had housed, had become a case. The number was 99–6750.

But this is Barbara McPhee's neck, Calista had to keep telling herself. O'Hare was speaking softly, almost gently.

"You see, when it's murder, the bruise mark goes straight across." He slid his finger in an imaginary line across the neck, parallel to the bottom of the page. "In a suicide, the marks look like an inverted V, just the way they do here. Look, you might be able to understand it better from this next picture." He took out a photograph from underneath. Calista swallowed. This picture showed more of the head. The jaw was completely exposed. Wisps of hair curled around her ear and the rope mark went straight up through these wisps and behind the ear. The jaw was cocked up to show the bruises. Calista leaned closer. The angle of that jaw was odd but familiar—not the angle so much as the pose. She closed her eyes briefly. She remembered those life-study drawing classes she had taken, years of drawing nude models. The models would hold the poses for as short as thirty seconds sometimes. It was an exercise in developing visual memory and skills in quick contour drawing. She had seen this pose before. Not in a life-drawing class, but in Barbara McPhee's living room: Bootsie sitting in the wing chair, her jaw tilted up as she leaned her head back, looking at the scrolls through half-closed eyes, twirling the ice in her drink with her index finger. And Gus, standing behind her, resting his hand on her shoulder. But he had to dip his hand down to rest it on her shoulder. For the back of the wing chair was high. And if . . .

"Are you okay, Ms. Jacobs?"

"Fine, just fine. But tell me one thing. Wouldn't an inverted V bruise be formed if someone was standing behind the victim, who was, say, sitting in a high-backed chair, and then slipped the rope down around her neck and then pulled up—presuming the victim's head was several inches lower than the murderer?"

"Yes."

"Then you have to look at the rope," Detective Froines said. "There should be abrasions on one side of the rope and you would see strands of the rope sticking out." She picked up a sheaf of papers and shook them slightly with a loose twist movement. "There is no report of that kind of abrasive action on the rope itself here. We check for that automatically." She looked steadily at Calista as if to say, I know my job, toots, and you are strictly an amateur.

This lady did have an attitude. But attitudes never undid Calista. She bit her lip slightly and concentrated on her next move. "You know, you're probably right. But that chair was upholstered in a silk brocade, an ivory on white. Silk is so smooth. It's hard imagining it roughing up a hemp rope like this. But the rope could certainly mess up the fabric of a chair like that—or at least rub it a little."

"That's a point," O'Hare said. "Lisa, why don't you and Bill go over to Brookline and take a look at the chair Ms. Jacobs is talking about. See if there are any rub marks, and in the meantime, maybe we should send this noose over to Michael and have him take a look at it through the electron microscope for foreign fibers."

Ha! thought Calista, and resisted looking triumphantly at Detective Froines. But she could not resist one last question.

"Might I go along with Detectives Froines and Graham?"

"I can't imagine how that would help," Froines said, looking to O'Hare. "I think we'll be able to find the chair in the living room on our own, Ms. Jacobs."

Bitch.

# 29

Calista had just driven through the two stone pillars that marked the entrance to St. Bennett's Academy. She checked her watch. Two hours and forty-five minutes from Boston. And the traffic hadn't been bad. She proceeded up the long, winding drive. There were signs directing visitors to the admissions office, administration, the athletic center. She took the turnoff for the athletic center. To the right of the parking lot, she saw tennis courts, but they were empty. She walked into the field house. It was elaborate. To think that Cambridge public schools had to cut back on hiring school librarians and this place had signs pointing to an ice-hockey rink, a Nautilus room, and another directing one downstairs to a swimming pool. The indoor tennis courts were apparently through the double doors directly ahead. There were several kids playing on the courts. A coach was watching carefully from the sidelines. There were some other kids sitting in the bleachers, holding racquets, apparently waiting their turn on the courts. Calista hoped that she wouldn't have to meet an adult. She could do this better with kids. She slid into the bleachers.

"Pardon me," she said to a young boy with tousled blond hair. "I'm looking for Gus Kingsley."

"Oh, Mr. Kingsley is only here on Tuesdays and Thursdays during the summer," the boy said.

"Oh dear . . . what a disappointment." She sighed. "I don't know whether I can get up here next Thursday, or Tuesday, for that matter. Do you know about what time he's apt to be here?"

"Ah well, he usually comes in the afternoon and stays overnight, because he lives all the way in Boston. Practice is from three till nine—we break for dinner."

"Oh," Calista said. "Does he go right back to Boston first thing in the morning on Fridays? I might be through here again on a Friday and could catch him."

"Jeez, I don't know. Sukey over there would have a better idea of when he's around. He's the custodian here."

Sukey spoke slightly more English than Calista spoke Japanese.

"Yes, yes, Mr. Gus always here Tuesday and Thursday . . . always . . . always. Never miss practice. Never miss practice." Sukey smiled broadly and swung his arms, mimicking a double-handed backhand. "I like to watch him myself. He can play with both hands. Velly good left or right!"

"Left or right!"

"Yah! Yah! Double backhand like Chris Evert."

Holy shit, Calista thought.

"Is he ever late?"

"Rate . . . no, no . . . bus rate sometimes. Yah, bus very rate Thursday. Kids must come from Manchester—and oh, there's Billy. Billy favorite of Mr. Gus. He tell you—me no speak so good English." He motioned Billy, a rather sullen-looking boy, over. "Billy is in dorm where Mr. Gus stay when here."

"Hello, Billy," Calista said. "I'm a friend of Gus Kingsley's and I can't seem to catch up with him. Apparently, I come the wrong days." She'd work into this easily and not ask Billy right off the bat whether Gus had been here last Thursday. She'd ask about other times first. "Tell me—I know he's always here on Thursday. Is there any chance of ever catching him very early on a Friday morning before he leaves?"

An absolutely distraught look passed over Billy's face. "Uh . . . I wouldn't know."

"Oh, I thought, since you were in his dorm . . ."

"My room is nowhere near his," he said fiercely. Calista blinked. The kid was desperate. This response was so out of kilter. She knew then instantly that he was lying. He had to be. She was as sure of this as she had been of anything in her life. But why would a kid in a summer program in a New Hampshire prep school lie or cover up for Gus Kingsley? How could a kid be involved with this? She must proceed very cautiously. The last thing she wanted to do was scare this kid off. But he was obviously very frightened.

"Well, oh no . . . I mean . . ." She ran her fingers through her hair in her best Mrs. Tiggy-Winkle fashion, hoping to look like something in between a kindly hedgehog and a distracted mother. She was very good on the latter. "I just thought I might be able to get through on Friday morning and catch him. But maybe a Thursday. Sukey was saying something about a late bus on Thursdays—"

Billy cut her off. "Sometimes the bus is late on Thursdays, but Mr. Kingsley is never late. He's always here. Always. I saw him myself last Thursday. He was here at five."

"Oh yes, yes, of course." Calista spoke mechanically. "Then maybe I'll try to be here then."

"Yes. He's always here on Thursdays."

The bus on Thursdays was apparently often late. Did this back up tennis practice and could Gus count on it being late? And why had Billy blurted out that he was here at five? She hadn't asked for a specific hour. Why five? Five was the estimated time of death of Barbara McPhee. It had said just that on the lab report from the crime lab. Right under the case number, there were two times: time of death, listed at 8:30 P.M., and estimated time of death—5:00 P.M. Eight-thirty was when Jamie had discovered his mother's body. Five was when Barbara had ceased to be Bootsie, had ceased to be a mother, and had become case number 99–6750.

# 30

When Calista got back to Boston, there was a message from Lieutenant O'Hare on the answering machine, asking her to call. She would have to hustle if she was to make drinks at 7:30 with Harley. And she didn't know whether Charley and Jamie were planning on eating at home this evening. They were supposed to have gotten the afternoon off from the swan boats because there was a private party that night and they were going to be working late. She'd leave money for them to order a pizza. She had begun to get undressed while being put on hold for Lieutenant O'Hare. When he finally picked up, she was naked and felt compelled for some idiotic reason to grab her robe from the back of the chair to cover up.

"Ms. Jacobs?"

"Yeah."

"You wanna come work for me?"

"How come?" she asked. She had put the robe on upside down and one sleeve was dragging on the floor.

"You were right. Somebody yanked her off. The back of that

chair had rope fibers and rub marks all over the edging material—you know, that fancy braid stuff they use to upholster the edges of furniture."

"Hah!" She tried not to gloat.

"You have any suspects in mind?"

"Yep."

"Who's that?"

"Her brother, Gus Kingsley."

"Why?"

"Well, he's ambidextrous for one thing." He can play tennis lefty or righty.

"But what would he use for murder? For yanking off his sister? We need something more concrete. A piece of physical evidence that would link him to the scene of the crime." Calista thought of the garter, but that, of course, was from the scene of a different crime. She wasn't quite ready to let that one go yet.

# 31

Charley looked up from the piece of paper. Jamie knew what was coming next. He wasn't sure if he could do it. "What did he do to you?"

Jamie wanted to say it was a long story, but that really wasn't the issue. It had started a while ago, but in many ways it was a simple story, now when Jamie looked back on it. It was a story of power and weakness. He had been ten and they had gone to Nohqwha for a fishing trip. Gus said it was part of being a man at Nohqwha. There had always been all sorts of secrets at Nohqwha and ceremonies. When you were six and could swim to the raft, you could go out in a canoe. When you could turn over the canoe and roll it back up, you could go out by yourself in it. When you were fourteen, you got to go duck hunting with the men in the fall. When you shot your first deer, they rubbed the blood on your head and threw you in the lake, if it wasn't frozen. These were weekends when no girls or women were allowed. Gus had shown him the sweat lodge that they had built just like the Indian ones and told him how the men sat naked in it and sweated out the impurities, especially the alcohol. Gus had said that the whole family drank too much. That he was smart and knew when to quit but that most people didn't. He hoped that Jamie wouldn't do that. He loved Jamie and had a lot of high hopes for him. He hoped that since Jamie's father had moved so far away, Jamie would come to think of Gus as a kind of father, someone whom he could always come to. And it would be his honor to raise Jamie in what he called the best of the Kingsley manly tradition. He used the word *manly* a lot. This was all part of being "manly," he had said—taking off your clothes and sitting naked in the woods, in the stone circles and in the Indian sweat lodge. This was how you must learn your body and its amazing powers.

So they would sit there and masturbate. That was how it had started, and then Gus would ask him to touch him. And when Jamie didn't want to, Gus had said, well, he would touch Jamie. He hadn't expected his uncle to do what he had done, to put it in his mouth. It didn't feel bad; it felt good. Then it had just gotten out of control and Gus had said that part of being a man was learning how to give pleasure; that he had learned how to give beautiful pleasure to his sisters. His father, Jamie's grandfather Kingie, had taught him. And his father before him had given pleasure. It was all part of a "manly" Kingsley tradition going way, way back. Jamie thought about all of this. How would he ever explain it to Charley. It was beyond comprehension. There was no explaining it. Better just say it.

His voice sounded very thin and far away, as if he were in space, in a place with no air, no atmosphere. "My uncle touched me, then he took my dick in his mouth, and then I took his, and then he raped me. And he's been doing it since I was about ten years old. And then my mom found out and she threatened to kill him and she went to Grandma and Grandma didn't believe her and then Grandma got killed and then my mom committed suicide and that's it."

Charley didn't know what to say. He felt his heart racing. He had heard about this kind of stuff; he'd read about it. But here was someone, a kid just his age, standing right in front of him telling him about it. He didn't know what do, what to say. He felt Jamie's shame. Yet another part of his brain was telling him in a very adult voice that there was no shame for Jamie in this. It wasn't his fault that he had been abused. But no matter, Charley knew that there had to be shame; he knew how he would feel—ruined, ruined for life, totally destroyed. He would want to die. He should be giving a pep talk to this kid. He should be telling him he had his whole life ahead of him; that he could put this behind him; that it was over; that he could grow up and be a productive citizen. Wasn't that what they always said? Wasn't that supposed to be the goal now for kids—a contributing member of society, of civilization? Productive citizen? It all sounded like such a load of crap now.

"Wh . . ." The word would not even come out whole. He started again. "Why did you tell me this?" Charley hoped it didn't sound like, Why me, poor little old me? But he was genuinely curious. And although not quite aware of it, implicit in the question was another one: What are we going to do here?

"I told you." Jamie spoke slowly. He was adjusting to this new feeling of letting his terrible secret out. He had told his mother, but it wasn't the same. She was so helpless and her outrage so futile. Her anger was more like a debilitating disease than anything else; it was just like her alcoholism. It ate at her. This felt better. Jamie began again. "I told you because I think that Gus is setting me up for something."

"It sounds from this letter that he's setting you up to take the rap for your grandmother's murder, or at least your mom thought so."

"Yeah, that's the point. I've thought a lot about this. I think that he wanted her to think that I did it and then maybe it would drive her so crazy that she would commit suicide and confess to it in order to cover up that I did it. My mom, you got to understand, spent half her life in a bottle of vodka. She could be made to believe almost anything and would get more and more paranoid the more she drank."

"You actually think that your uncle could have convinced her that her own son killed his grandmother?"

"Not convinced her, but scared her shitless."

"But I don't understand. What motive could he have manufactured, or you?"

"None for me, but I think he had plenty."

"You mean you think that he murdered your grandmother?"

"Yes."

"What was his motive? Why would he want to do it?"

"Money—money and the fear that my mom would really blow the whistle on what he had done to me. She had already told Grandma and I think Grandma was on the brink of changing her will to give a lot more to Mom than she had planned to. This was really earthshaking, because Gus had always been Grandma's favorite. And to tell you the truth, I'm not sure if Grandma was that upset about what he had done to me. I don't think she believed it. At least that was the sense I got from Mom."

"Then if she didn't believe it, why would she change her will to favor your mother?"

"Because my mom was threatening to make a stink in public; she was going to go to a lawyer, and not that idiot Harley Bishop. She was going to go to the DA. That really scared the shit out of Grandma. Grandma Queenie believed that there were only about three times when a person should get their names in the paper. When they were born, when they got married, and when they died."

Charley whistled low. This was incredible. "So you think that in order to shut up your mom, she was going to buy her off?"

"Yes."

"But you said your mom was tanked half the time. How did she get it together even to think about the DA and go to your grandmother and read her the riot act? I mean, that takes a certain amount of sobriety."

"Mom had her clear periods. She had a clear one starting in late spring—May, June, well into July. She was determined to do something about this. But then I don't know, she just kind of started crumbling again."

"So let me get this straight. You think that your grandma really would have changed her will to avoid publicity?"

"Yes."

"But if she had changed it, wouldn't that have given your mom a motive? I mean, then she could have gotten all the money before your grandma changed it again. You know, she did that all the time." Charley quickly bit his lip.

"How do you know?" Jamie said. His voice was shot through with tension.

There was no beating around this one. Charley knew it. He had blabbed too much. "Because I hacked into Hopkins, Bishop and Creeth's computers. Your Uncle Rudy asked me to."

"You did?" Jamie was stunned. "Uncle Rudy asked you?"

"Yep."

"What did you find?"

"That your grandmother changed her will about as often as some people change their socks. And in the last will, we found everything was in your uncle's favor still."

"It was?"

"Yep. You want to see?"

Charley walked over to the desk in his bedroom. He booted up his computer and punched in the numbers on the keypad of the telephone. For twenty minutes, they read through the various letters, wills, and amendments to wills that composed Quintana Kingsley's file at Hopkins, Bishop and Creeth. Charley leaned forward suddenly and peered harder at the screen.

"There's something new."

"New?"

"Well, at least I don't remember seeing this when Rudy and I were going through the file the other day. It's dated August 1."

"That's two days before Grandma died. Open it up."

Charley and Jamie read the short letter from Quintana Kingsley to Harley Bishop requesting the following amendments to her will so that the bulk of her estate be held in an irrevocable trust for her only grandson, Jamie, with his mother and Rudy Kingsley as the principal executors. The last part of the letter glared on the screen.

> For reasons that I do not want to go into in this letter, or at any future time, I think that this is the best arrangement for all parties considered. I know this is a move that Rudy had urged Kingie to make years ago. There is no fool like an old fool, and Rudy is no fool. I am afraid that perhaps I have had the dubious honor of having been both an old and a young fool throughout my life. I can never make amends at this late date for past errors, but I can try to avoid making new errors. I shall be in first thing Friday morning to sign the papers necessary for the irrevocable trust and the newly amended will. Sincerely yours, Quintana Kingsley.

Charley looked up at Jamie.

"She was dead by Friday morning," he said quietly.

"Yes. So it remained unsigned and the last will, dated July twenty-seventh, was the one in which Gus got it all."

"We've got to tell Rudy this," Charley said.

"And we have to tell Rudy the rest, too," Jamie said quietly.

# 32

There were a lot of horses' asses at the Ritz bar, most of them hanging on the wall, jumping hedges. However, it could have been worse. Calista was always happy that the Ritz bar was not one of those places that went in for paintings of drooling dogs and bleeding pheasants. The portraiture in general tended to favor well-groomed lapdogs—terriers, corgis, the occasional dachshund. The portraits of people had a marked affinity for the austere—a Thoreau-like young man looking simultaneously contemplative and ethereal due to a particularly wan pallor. This gentleman faced a Hawthornesque Puritan maiden walking through a woods. The picture always reminded Calista of the scene in *The Scarlet Letter* where Hester and Dimsdale finally had words seven years after having nookie.

The best thing about the Ritz bar was that it was one of those rare places that seemed to be a little universe unto itself, a tiny independent solar system, totally oblivious to any other gravitational systems or forces. It had its own unique light, a warm, redolent amber glow; its own weather, crisp yet warm; its own season, forever autumn.

She spotted Harley Bishop in a far corner. He stood up as he saw her coming across the room. He had already ordered a drink, a martini. Despite his horn-rimmed glasses and button-downed demeanor, there was a look of clear anticipation on his face. It was not just sexual. This guy wanted more. Calista had sensed it immediately from the first time she'd met him, in the rain on Louisburg Square. This guy was looking for someone to change his life. He was the late George Apley waked up and realizing that although he had done everything just the way it should be done, maybe just maybe, he should have considered an alternative.

Alas, Calista had neither the time nor the inclination for this kind of rehab work. She had already begun to pity the poor woman who would eventually take Harley on and the poor wife he would most likely be leaving behind or hurting in some way despite the best of intentions. A little dirge to be sung for such lives. Calista remembered now the part from the Marquand novel when Apley questioned his very existence. Fragments of those lines came back: " 'Have any of us really lived?' he asked. 'Sometimes I am not entirely sure; sometimes I think that we are all amazing people, placed in an ancestral mould. . . . [But] There is no spring, no force'."

"Hello, Calista. I am so glad you've come." Harley Bishop reached for her hand as if she was extending a lifeline.

Their drinks came, a second martini for Harley, a Campari and soda for Calista.

"Well, here's to!" Harley lifted his glass and she, to be polite, did the same. But what were they drinking to? And why in the hell was she here? Why was he here, for that matter? He was married. And Calista herself was as good as married to Archie. Well, she knew why she was here. It was not because she was horny. It was because she wanted to find out all she could from Harley about the Kingsleys, starting with Gus. How to begin? But he was already beginning.

"I went over to Barnes and Noble today and looked at your books. They are quite marvelous."

"Thank you."

"I was wondering . . ."

"Yes?"

"Sometimes, I almost felt that I was catching a glimpse of you in an illustration, but just rarely. Do you ever draw yourself in?"

"All the time."

"How fascinating. I was right, then. I thought I saw a little bit of you in the eyes of the cat in *Puss 'N Boots.*"

"Oh yes, that's my most obvious appearance in any of my books."

"Well, where else?"

"Oh, you have to look hard." Calista smiled. Her hooded dark eyes crinkled. Harley leaned forward. There was something very spellbinding about her eyes, glinting with a kind of sorcery that seemed to come from another world—a world of gnomes and giants and evil fairies.

"Well, where should I look?"

"Sometimes in the scariest and ugliest parts of the pictures." He realized she was dead serious. He took a big swallow of his martini and set it down. "Did you see my book *Snow White?*"

"Yes, yes. I do believe I did. Were you one of the Seven Dwarfs?"

"Oh no, worse." Calista laughed. Again the dark eyes sparkled, full of merriment. "Remember the evil stepmother?"

"You weren't her?"

"Oh no—she was pure Leona Helmsley. Well, with a touch of Nancy Reagan for leavening purposes. But remember her mirror?"

"The mirror?" Harley said vaguely. "You mean when she says 'Mirror mirror on the wall'?"

"Yeah, the frame."

"The frame?" His brow knitted.

A child would have never missed this, but a person who spent seven hours a day doing estate law might. "Yeah, the frame was made to look as if it was carved. It had all those death's-heads and . . . well, some sort of suggestive phallic shapes, lots of writhing bodies—very Hieronymus Bosch."

"You're in the frame."

"Yep, one of the death's-heads. Look in the forest, in the bark of some of the tree trunks. You'll see me there, too—same death's-head just transposed to the bark of the tree."

"My, my! You're a very interesting person."

Calista smiled warmly. "No, I'm really not, not at all. You see, I get all my fantasies out and down on paper—in ink and gouache and watercolor and acrylics. What's more interesting and more dangerous are the folks who don't." She paused. Harley looked nervously into his drink, as if wishing that the olive sitting in the vortex of the glass would suddenly jump up and say something. "Folks like the Kingsleys," Calista added.

"I'm not following your drift here, Calista."

Go for it! a little voice in the back of her mind seemed to mutter, and the voice was not hers, but Archie's. Time to call a spade a spade, Cal. "Did you know that generations of Kingsley children, girls, and young women have been sexually abused throughout their younger lives by Kingsley men?"

Harley blanched. His lips began to tremble. "As legal counsel for the Kingsley family, I must caution you before you proceed any further with this discussion or these accusations."

"Who's going to sue me? Kingie Kingsley? He's dead. As is his father, Tad, who passed on this marvelous tradition. The victims, too, except for Titty, are dead."

"Titty—was abused?"

"Yes. She told me herself. And Rudy knows about it all."

"Rudy knows?"

"Yes. But I really didn't come here to discuss that." Harley seemed to sag in anticipation of something worse. "I don't think that Barbara McPhee killed herself."

"Bootsie didn't commit suicide?"

"Harley,"—Calista leaned forward—"I don't want to sound melodramatic about any of this, but could we call her Barbara? She hated that name Bootsie. Bootsie is like a name you give a pet. I happen to think that Barbara was a real person, although her family never treated her that way. So I just feel better calling her Barbara."

Harley's eyes looked steadily into Calista's. Then he settled back into his chair and stared down at his knee. He looked totally forlorn and depressed, deeply depressed. He had come to this meeting with such anticipation, such excitement. His own life had become so vapid with Joanie; his work life so constricting; his children so removed. He didn't even know what love was anymore. Or had he ever? Then on that dreary rainy day on Louisburg Square, this woman had appeared, as tantalizing as any creature Ulysses had encountered, with her wild silvery hair and hooded eyes full of sorcery. She had appeared like the sexual witch that had haunted their musty Puritan past, a glorious succubus. God, he had ached whenever he thought of her. And now here she sat, still beautiful in this very odd way, but so sensible, and not righteous, but just and wise in ways he never dreamed. Nothing scared her, either. He had just threatened her—well, warned her—that he was legal counsel from the most distinguished of all Boston law firms for one of the oldest of Brahmin families and she hadn't flinched. Rather, she'd very politely reminded him that the perpetrators of these abuses were dead, as were all the victims save for Titty. Harley Bishop had thought he was going to come to this meeting at the Ritz and maybe change his life. That wasn't going to be, and she had told him a worse tale. What was that she was saying now?

"I don't think she killed herself. I think that Gus killed her."

"Gus?"

She had to work carefully now. She could not reveal that Charley had busted into Hopkins, Bishop and Creeth's computer.

"Would he have stood to gain anything from his mother's immediate death?"

Yes, thought Harley, everything if Quintana Kingsley died before the meeting in his office on that Friday morning, as indeed she had.

# 33

"Madame X, how delightful to hear your voice. I'm so sorry to have had to rush you off earlier. But all to your benefit, my dear."

Leon Mauritz signaled his secretary, who immediately put through a call to a number in Boston.

In a private room at the Harvard Club, Rudy Kingsley stood with four distinctly scroungy young men whom Malcolm had let in through the rear door that afternoon. When the phone rang, it was as if a current had passed through the five people. Charley, Jamie, and Liam stood in a semicircle around a man in his late twenties seated in front of Charley's laptop. This was Phink Tank, the hottest phone phreak in the Northeast. Like many phone phreaks, Phink Tank had worked deep in the bowels of the baby bells as a consultant. He was an expert in AT&T hardware and digital communications. Since college, he had been the local technical backup for the AT&T 3B2 system, a monster multiuser UNIX platform 3 with 3.2 gigabytes of storage. Phink Tank knew this system in and out; he was legendary for his expertise. He had written an elegant code-scanning program by the time he was eighteen and he was, to boot, a wily operator. For years, since the break up of Ma Bell, he had been sucking away at AT&T and UNIX. He had a mess of corporate code, but he never sold it for a penny. He was an electronic Robin Hood—stealing from the monolithic pavilions of phone technology and redistributing it among the poor, passing around a source code that supposedly was kept under well-guarded security but that in reality was about as effective as a rusty chastity belt on Madonna. But most important, he was quiet about his underground work.

As a consultant at AT&T, he was adequately paid but got no benefits, no insurance, no retirement program—no nothing. He hated the idea of intellectual property; he hated these fat cats. He didn't cause harm like Fry Guy, but he liked playing Robin Hood with software.

Of course, if the company had found out, they would have been outraged. He was a "field niggah" in the company and he was supposed to come in through the back door and not eat with the good silver. Tonight, he sat in the Harvard Club and when the call came through from Leon Mauritz's office, he began his fine dance through the switching stations. He punched a few more buttons on his phone keypad. Within nanoseconds, he was into the system as a technician.

"These Centrex lines are incredibly insecure. They operate off of standard UNIX software and this new generalized automatic remote thing—the one they call GARDEN—is a crock. You don't even need a trashy Radio Shack One Thousand to reprogram the switching station. You just log on as I have done here, as a technician. Okay, listen up."

Leon Mauritz's voice came through a box. "I have a prospective buyer, very enthusiastic."

"Oh really!" the female voice trilled. Rudy's brow creased. It was not a voice he had ever heard before.

"Who is this man?" the voice asked.

"What makes you think it's a man?" Leon replied. There was a pause. One could almost sense the caller's surprise. "It is," Mauritz said quickly. "I just don't think we should jump to conclusions about these things."

"Right, of course." But there was a quaver in the voice that had not been there before.

"This person insists on seeing the netsukes within the next forty-eight hours." Rudy lifted a triumphant fist and shook it in the air. Leon was coming through just as he knew he would.

"Oh . . ." Another pause.

"Is there some problem?"

"No . . . this is just rather sudden and I hadn't expected things to happen so quickly."

"Well, where are you? My client is prepared to fly anyplace."

More hesitation. "Uh . . . New York . . ."

Rudy's eyebrows shot up.

"Good. Let's say day after tomorrow. My office at four P.M."

"No. I shall call and tell you where by four o'clock."

"Fine. Just as long as it's within the next twenty-four hours."

"He better be serious."

"Madame, I don't deal with people who aren't."

"Well, tomorrow, then. You'll hear from me. Good-bye." There was a click as the caller hung up and the connection was severed.

"I got the number. It's a seven-two-three exchange. That's Boston; maybe Back Bay."

# 34

Calista walked out of the Ritz bar, heading diagonally across the Public Garden toward Charles Street. She wasn't sure Harley had believed her. But maybe it didn't really matter. It seemed as if Lieutenant O'Hare was beginning to. Her head swirled with thoughts. She paused to look at the beds of tuberous begonias. They were thick and velvety, brilliant crimsons and magentas. She did not notice the simply dressed but elegant woman stopped at the opposite bed to admire the evening primrose. Calista began walking again. The woman followed.

Calista thought about Billy. She was sure he was lying. But why would a kid in a summer program in a New Hampshire prep school lie or cover up for Gus Kingsley? How could a kid be involved with this? Unless. . . . She stopped in her tracks. Children, young people, had always been abused by Kingsley men. Was it possible that? Astonishment crept into her slowly but surely. With an inexorable certainty she began to feel a new truth.

She was at the far corner of the gardens. Bronze ducks were set in the asphalt path to commemorate the Robert McCloskey classic children's book *Make Way for Ducklings.* The elegantly dressed woman paused near a bed with concentric circles of gaily colored petunias when Calista stopped. Is it possible, thought Calista, that Gus is abusing this boy? And if he is doing that, could he have done something to Jamie, as well? She lifted her hand toward her mouth. The possibility of this truth was awful. Was there no end to it all? The woman's shadow slid up behind her. Calista took off jogging. She must call Rudy. She must tell Lieutenant O'Hare to go out to St. Bennett's.

Calista was very good at running in heels. The woman was not.

# 35

He couldn't believe that he was doing this at his age. But then again, wasn't that precisely the point? His age. Eighty-one years. It had been a good life. Wonderful friends, some truly splendid lovers, and pots of money. He had nothing to lose, but they had so much to lose. And Jamie, poor boy! Still, they would call him a fool for trying this. But he was an old man now and he did not want young, innocent people getting hurt.

It had been sticky with Calista. She had wanted to know why he couldn't meet with her immediately. But if he had told her, she would have wanted to come along. She was that kind—a tad reckless. She had told him about what the police had discovered about the so-called suicide. Very clever of her. Now as he sat crouched behind the standing Edo screen, his back began to hurt. He had taken two Motrin already. God, getting old was a pain. He had selected the camouflage of the screen because from it one could see the living room, the front hall, and the staircase going to the second floor. Rudy had had a hunch that at least one of the netsukes was here and not at Gus's place. Here where

Bootsie would never find it, but where he could have arranged for the cops to find it—that is before he became aware of how much the pair together would be worth. So Rudy was prepared to wait it out for Gus. And then what? He had tried to get through to the police, the Lieutenant O'Hare Calista had mentioned. His best hope would be to get through this next part with no confrontation. He had brought an old revolver that he'd found over at Queenie's just in case things got dicey. Of course, the thing looked like something left over from the Crimean War.

If he could just confirm that it was indeed Gus, then follow him to New York and the meeting with Mauritz. By that time, good God, he should be able to get through to the police. Ah! A noise—the distinct sound of a key turning in the lock. He heard footsteps. They were coming into the front hall.

Rudy blinked, but he wasn't fooled for a moment by the heels, cream-colored pleated skirt, and matching linen jacket. The hips appeared very slender, the shoulders wide, and the calves muscular as the figure mounted the stairs. It was Gus. He should have known that Gus might have this bent. Hadn't Kingie started to get very naughty at those Welles Club "Frivolities," almost to the point of embarrassment on the part of some of the other members? Seemed like Kingie had liked keeping the clothes on a little too long after the event and began some rather embarrassing flirtations with Albie Belmont's youngest boy.

There was a ring at the doorbell. Rudy froze. Who in the world could that be? What was supposed to happen now? He certainly hadn't planned on this contingency. He wondered if Gus had. Would he open the door? There was no sound from upstairs. But then once more, he heard the click of the lock's tumblers.

"Yoo-hoo! Rudy, are you here?"

Good Lord, it was Calista Jacobs! "I got this extra key from Titty."

"Oh . . . oh my . . . I'm sorry. . . ." Calista looked at the top of the stairs. There was a woman in a cream-colored suit. She began coming down the stairs toward Calista. Then it all seemed to happen very quickly. Fragments of images swirled through her brain like the bits of colored glass in a kaleidoscope. A pattern arose. There was the picture of the Welles Club men all tarted up for the "Frivolities." There was Kingie with the hourglass waist—he wore it so well, Titty had said. And so had the lady in the green-house, the lady with the garter! Like father, like son. The realization exploded in Calista's brain. This was no lady. This was Gus and he was going to kill her.

# 36

"You just couldn't stay away, could you?"

Calista was thinking as fast as she could. She had to convince him that he would never get away with this, that too many people already knew.

What could she say? Where to begin? Could she pretend that the cops knew everything for sure? That there was plenty of evidence? She'd just have to wing it.

"You know . . . uh . . . you don't think anybody knows about you, do you?" She didn't wait for an answer. Just keep talking. Every word, every syllable meant delay; delay was good. "You gotta think this through, Gus."

"You have to think it through, Calista!" he said, moving toward her.

"No . . . no . . . you don't get it. Everybody knows, you see, Gus, just everybody. They know you killed Queenie. And . . . uh . . . they know about the money, all that stuff with Harley Bishop and the will, and the cops got the picture fast on Barbara's death. They've got it all figured out, Gus. They've got evidence." She was almost panting. It felt more like sprinting than talking, but it might have to be a long-distance race.

"Like what kind of evidence?"

She shouldn't say they had prints. He might have been wearing gloves. She thought fast.

"Fiber stuff . . . it's not like fiber optics that they do; it's this other kind of fiber stuff . . . you . . . you . . ." she stammered. "You left fucking fibers all over the place!" She almost shouted the words.

"She's right, Gus." Both their heads swiveled as Rudy stepped out from behind the screen, holding the gun. In one swift gesture, Gus tore off his wig, threw it right into Rudy's face, and lunged, knocking Rudy down like a paper doll. Gus had the gun and, wheeling around, he grabbed Calista. "Rudy!" Calista screamed. A thin trickle of blood seeped from just above his ear. Had he been shot? She hadn't heard anything. Suddenly, she was aware of this excruciating pain in her arm. Gus had it twisted up behind her.

"You're coming with me."

"Where?"

"That's your car."

"Yes."

It was close to midnight. There was not a soul out on the streets. He was immensely strong.

"I want Jamie."

"I don't know where he is."

"I do."

"Where?"

"He's finishing up at the gardens. Probably wiping down the swan boats—late party, right?" He laughed harshly. "See, I'm no dunce. I figure things out."

"Oh yeah!"

He took the butt end of the gun and knocked her in the jaw. It hurt worse than anything she could imagine. Her whole face and the inside of her skull clenched in a spasm of fierce pain. She tasted blood.

"No smart remarks, Calista. Else you die now and I get the kids later."

She could hardly register what he was saying through the pain. Did he say "kids"? Was he going after Charley, too? They were walking down the front steps toward her car. He was opening the door. He had wrestled her into her car.

"Where are your keys?"

"In my sweater pocket."

He jammed his hand into the pocket and took out the keys.

"Okay, now drive!"

"I can't!"

"What do you mean you can't?"

Her words sounded thick and far away. "I hurt too much." Her whole face hurt so badly, she could not move it.

"You will!" He pointed the gun at her temple. She started the car and pulled away from the curb. He sat close to her, the gun thrust just under her throat. He helped her steer with his other hand.

The pain was unbearable. She could not think, let alone talk.

But time played funny tricks. She couldn't remember the route or the drive. But suddenly, they were there, at the gardens. It was after midnight. She was being propelled along the path toward the pond. There were a few people out for a late night stroll, but did she and Gus look any different? He had the gun pressed against the small of her back. He was rasping in her ear. The words came out in a hot, rapid-fire way. He was telling her what to do. How did he know the boys would still be there? She wasn't sure herself. The party was definitely over, but the swan boats were not tied at the far end where they left them for the night. That meant that the cleanup crew was still working. Charley and Jamie and Matthew were the cleanup crew. They got paid extra for it. So they would be here.

Gus had figured everything out. There was a growing sense of dread welling up from the pit of her stomach. She stumbled. He yanked her up. She had just one thought: She could not allow anything to happen to the kids. Nothing. She would kill before she allowed those kids to be harmed. She would not only kill; she would die for those kids. She had all to lose and nothing to gain—unlike Gus, who had all to gain and nothing to lose. The thought gave her a strange comfort. There was some sort of peculiar logic to it that made her feel superior, stronger—more ready for the fight. Now what the hell was he saying?

"You have to go over there and call to Jamie." She could barely talk let alone call out. "And remember, I'm going to be right behind you in those bushes. I'm a good shot, Calista. And don't worry—I won't shoot you; I'll shoot Charley."

Her pain dissolved instantly and a rage began to creep through her. They were near the entrance to the swan-boat pier.

"You got that?"

"Yeah," she mumbled. Her teeth felt as if they were swimming in blood.

She walked through the gate and was just stepping onto the pier. She could see the boys mopping down the boats.

"Mom?" Charley said, looking up.

"Get down, Charley!" she screamed.

There was a huge blast, an acrid smell. She saw Charley fall backward into the water.

"Charley!" she screamed, and ran toward the boat. She heard a click, then another. Two of her teeth hit the pier. Then it was chaos. Gus came charging out of the bushes. Matthew and Jamie ducked for cover. Calista was on her belly, sprawled across the floor of a swan boat.

# 37

The sergeant and his partner looked at the old queer sitting in the wing chair and wondered who in the hell he had tried to pick up. Wearily, Rudy began to explain again.

"Look, I don't have time for this nonsense. I tell you that nothing has been stolen—except the two netsukes."

"What?"

Oh God, why had he mentioned that? Now he was going to have to give a lecture on Japanese art to this none-too-bright-looking boy in uniform. "I am telling you that this is the home of my late niece, who was murdered. But on the police files, it said it was suicide, apparently until this morning when Lieutenant O'Hare confirmed my friend's suspicions."

"O'Hare?"

"Yes, Lieutenant O'Hare, and there is a Detective Brant who is working on the case of my sister-in-law."

"What case is that?"

"Mrs. Elliot Kingsley. She was murdered a few weeks ago."

"The Beacon Hill case."

"Yes!" There was a flicker of light in the young cop's eyes. Two neurons connecting, Rudy prayed. "I'm telling you there is a crime in progress right now. This lovely woman has been abducted by a homicidal maniac—my nephew. I don't know where they went, but he is terribly dangerous."

"I'll put in a call to unit Three-four."

"And try to get O'Hare."

Rudy had come to just as he heard Calista's car drive away. He had sat up and tried to put his thoughts in order. He was still trying to put his thoughts in order as he followed the two cops down the steps of Bootsie's house.

"You say you are staying at the Harvard Club?"

"Yes, but why?"

"We'll take you back there after we take you over to Mass General."

"Why in the world would you be taking me to Mass General?"

"That gash is going to need some stitches. In a man of your age, it might be more serious than you think, sir."

"And who cares if it is? I am eighty-one years old. Can I not impress on you two young gentlemen the importance of finding this maniac? He has kidnapped somebody."

"Well, we've called it in."

"Look, fellows, I don't care if I die. But we have to move fast. Listen to me for just a second." He touched the younger cop's lapels in an infinitely gentle way. The cop found himself strangely moved by this man's selflessness, a selflessness that he seldom encountered in his job.

# 38

"Charley!" Calista scanned the water. Where could he be? The pond was barely three feet deep. Then she saw him. "Charley!" His head was above the water.

"Don't worry, Mom. I'm okay. I felt something hit me, but I'm not bleeding. It just knocked me off the boat. But God, you are! What happened to you? You've got blood all over your face."

"Charley," she whispered hoarsely, "it's Gus. He's after us, all of us. He's totally insane. He's got a gun." She suddenly heard the creak and wash of the pier.

"I'm coming after you. Goddamn it. Jamie! Jamie!" Gus shouted in a hoarse voice.

"Quick, get in the water, Mom!"

Calista slipped over the side. The water felt cold. But it was not very deep. She had to crouch. She saw Jamie and Matthew under the stern of the boat ahead. Then she saw the boat suddenly lurch. Gus had stepped on it. The boys seemed to disappear.

"Where'd they go?" Calista whispered.

"Under the paddle wheel, between the two pontoons. There's a groove. We've got to do it, too."

She felt Charley dunk her and then pull her into a space. She broke through the water. Their heads seemed to be in a dark box between the two pontoons that formed the understructure of the swan boat. The boat began to rock wildly.

"You're here! You're here! I know you're here," Gus cried, then he jumped to another boat.

Charley stared at his mom. She could see his horror over her appearance. But she was curiously detached. She didn't even feel the pain in her jaw anymore. But the gears in her mind were starting to click in, take hold. Was it possible that the gun had blanks? Charley had said he had been hit, but he wasn't bleeding. She drew closer to Charley. She cupped her hands over his ear. "Where were you hit?" she whispered.

Charley then cupped his hands over her ear. "My left shoulder. But it just aches a little."

She felt down the left side of his neck to his shoulder. "Right there!" Charley whispered. "I think it was the surprise that made me fall rather than the bullet."

Calista thought he might be right. Then Charley, enveloped by his mother's growing calm, became curiously detached, too. He was thinking. He was contemplating cause and effect and the convention of linear events as they are linked through cause and effect. But Charley remembered his father talking about oddities of time; places where time flowed backward or raindrops were suspended for eternities and never hit the ground; occasions when cause and effect became separated and no longer were part of a logical conjunction. Places that disobeyed the known laws of physics and time, like black holes. Perhaps he and his mom had fallen into one of those 'tween places.

It was very odd. Calista had always wondered how she might act in a situation like this. This calm that followed the shock was mesmerizing, and strangest of all, she felt the presence of Tom. Had it been just barely a month ago that she had been so depressed about missing him, missing him forever? It seemed weird. Why miss him when he seemed so near? He did seem near. She must think now and not just revel in his nearness.

The gun had not shot Charley. Yet they were proceeding as if it had. Cause and effect had been disrupted, disjointed. This was one of those universes that Tom had lectured to his students about in the core-curriculum physics course. It was the lecture following the one about special relativity, which explained the ins and outs of Einstein's theory as it related to such phenomena as time dilation, which occurred when one was traveling near light speed. Tom would give a lecture called "Jacob's Weird Places," in which he would upset all notions of conventional physics, including relativity, and begin to imagine realms where time stopped altogether, or flowed backward, or where time was not at all linear, or never a quantity at all, but a quality. Calista felt she had entered one of Tom's weird places. And he was right beside her.

Once more, she cupped her hand over Charley's ear. "I'm going out. I'm going to distract him. Can you get through this groove to where Matthew and Jamie are?"

Charley nodded.

"Okay, now listen. When you hear me start carrying on, you boys make a run for it. There's got to be a cop around here someplace."

Charley felt calm. His mother was doing just what she should. She was reversing the cause-effect cycle. He could picture it just like the boxes in a cartoon sequence. Box number one: Charley gets blown into the water. Box number two: His mom blows out of the water; the gun would turn back, the gunfire be redirected.

Calista had ducked under and out of the paddle-wheel box. It was very hard to swim in such shallow water. She only needed to get over to the shore just beyond the pier. She was almost there. The concrete sides of the pond began to slope upward. She staggered out. She could see Gus still on the boats. He stood sleek and dark among the swans' gracefully curving necks.

"Help! Police!" she yelled at the top of her lungs. Gus wheeled around. She raced across the grass. He came running toward her. She swerved at a statue and then headed toward Charles Street. God, he was gaining on her. No wonder. She was drenched, her sneakers full of water. She didn't dare take time to kick them off. It was only one hundred feet to the corner of Beacon and Charles. She heard a tremendous grunt and something hit the pavement behind her. She turned to look. "God Bless Robert McCloskey!" she muttered through her mouth, dribbling blood and bits of teeth. He had tripped on a bronze duckling and was flat on the ground. She kept running.

Then she heard shots. And the night was illuminated with blue flashing lights. Calista stopped. She was confused. "Tom!" she called softly. She was trembling. The flash of glitter and blue light limned the trees. There were cars on the grass. How odd. Right by the KEEP OFF THE GRASS sign, there were three cars with sirens. The world had dissolved into absolute chaos. "Tom?" she called again. But he was gone and there was this strange little elfin man coming up to her, putting his arms around her.

"It's all over, Calista. Sergeant, bring me a blanket, please, and yes, call an ambulance . . . She seems to be bleeding from her mouth. Don't worry, dear. Charley's here. Jamie's here. The boy Matthew is here."

But Calista was crying. Oh, how she missed Tom again. She would have to go on missing him for the rest of her life. He had been with her. He had!

And then she remembered nothing.

# 39

There is a special glory to an early-autumn day with the crispness in the air and the light refulgent and golden, gilding every blade of grass and rimming every cloud in a shimmer. Calista reclined on the wicker chaise lounge in her newly finished conservatory and looked at a plant her mother had sent her, hoping to goodness she could keep this one alive. The light fell through glass panels onto the jewel-colored octagonal tiles. The plumber was supposed to come today and hook up the little pool, which she preferred to call a "grotto" at the other end of the room. Charley couldn't wait to buy goldfish for it and she herself had ordered some waterlilies, a particularly hearty variety that she had read about in *Horticulture* magazine. She thought about Jamie. His father had shown up quicker than they had anticipated and he seemed genuinely grieved by Barbara's death and Jamie's own particular tragedy. But most important, Jamie seemed really pleased to see his dad. He had left with him just the day before yesterday to begin a new life, hopefully a much better life, in California.

Calista looked around the room. It had turned out nicely and it would be lovely in all seasons, but especially come January, when it would offer a sunny oasis in the long New England winter. At this point, Calista couldn't wait for winter—for winter and for Archie. He was supposed to be coming home in two days. She had refused to let Charley or the elder Baldwins call Archie or bring him home early. It was ridiculous. He was supposed to be home within a week after the frightful events in the Public Garden. No sense getting him all upset. Everything was fine, after all—well, almost fine. Calista took the glass of lemonade and delicately slid the special straw through her teeth. There were a few gaps now. That made it easier.

She heard someone coming in through the front part of the house. It must be the plumber, she thought. Charley had stuck around to let him in. She took a sip and went back to her book, *Barchester Towers*. She wondered whether she could be hauled around on this rig à la Signorini Neroni. She was feeling quite languorous and almost Italian in this setting, what with her grotto about to be hooked up.

"Hello!"

Calista looked up over her reading glasses.

Archie!

Only it came out "Awshie."

Certain consonants were impossible with her jaw wired shut. She started to raise herself from the chaise, but then Archie was there all over her, cradling her head, her fragile Humpty-Dumpty head, in his arms, kissing her face.

"Tell me where it doesn't hurt . . . so I can kiss you."

"It dushn't matter. Kish me where it hurz. Kish me all over."

This was heaven. She buried her cheek in his neck and smelled him. He smelled so good, and the wonderful blue eyes, crinkled, slightly tired, full of worry, worry for her. His rough short gray-brown hair scratched her forehead. She pushed him away and ran her fingers over his face. She couldn't quite believe it. But here he was, every wonderful bit of him. How often she had drawn those great cheekbones, cheekbones to die for, the angular jaw, the gentle slope of the eyelids. Oh God! She was one lucky woman.

"There was this package outside for you."

It was postmarked from England. "Oh, it mush be frum Rudy."

"Rudy?"

"Long story." Calista opened it. There was a narrow box.

"Turnbull & Asser. My goodness," said Archie.

She lifted the lid and unfolded the tissue paper. There was a beautiful pink shirt and an ascot, the colors of which could only be described as rhubarb and custard. She took a card out of the envelope.

> I figured you were about my size. So they made one up, a "bespoke shirt," as they say, for a dear friend and in the colors of the regiment to which another dear friend of mine belonged.
>
> With much love, Rudy.

"Ah, how schweet." Calista sighed. Then she caught sight of something by Archie's leg. She had remembered him carrying a box when she had first looked up from her book.

"Whassh dat?"

"A rare orchid, my dear, from the rain forest."

Calista's neck turned red. Archie loved to watch Calista blush. It always started as a red flare on her neck and crept toward her jaw—her poor old jaw.

"The one you shaid reminded you of me—"

"Certain parts."

"Oh boy, Awshie."

"Yes, darling, a dirty mind is a joy forever!" He kissed her again.

That evening, before they got down to dirty, Archie brought out a bottle of Veuve Cliquot that he had put on ice. Veuve Cliquot was Calista's favorite champagne. She had always loved it, even before she became a widow. Nobody had noticed then. But Archie knew how the widow loved the Veuve and he had made sure to stop on his way from the airport and get the Grand Dame. The most distinguished of all the *cuvées* in its fetchingly curvaceous black bottle. Charley joined them. Archie poured the sparkling liquid into three glasses. Calista slipped a straw into hers. They lifted their glasses in a silent toast. They took their sips. It was wonderful.

She closed her eyes and savored it in the back of her mouth for a second before swallowing. She thought how lucky she was to be drinking this champagne in the company of all these good men— all three.

"Still good with the straw?"

She remembered the words of the old monk Dom Perignon on the occasion when he first tasted the liquid he had invented.

"Issh like drinking the schtars! I mean . . ." She paused. "Stars!"

She said the word with painful clarity.

The Date Due Card in the pocket indi-
cates the date on or before which this
book should be returned to the Library.
Please do not remove cards from this
pocket.